FIGHTING FOR BERLIN

Redemption Harbor Security, #5

Katie Reus

DEDICATION

For my mom.

CHAPTER 1

*The only person you have to live with is
yourself.*

Berlin turned down the radio as Bradford steered into her sister's apartment complex.

"Thank god," Bradford muttered. They'd become friends years ago, back when they'd both worked for Redemption Harbor Security in North Carolina. Now they worked out of the New Orleans location and he was still one of her favorite people.

"What?" She glanced at him before scanning the parking lot out of habit. She hadn't always been as vigilant about her surroundings, but now it was second nature to be aware of everything around her.

"Nothing...just glad you turned down the volume."

She blinked. "Oh my god, when did you become an old man?"

He lifted a shoulder, grinned. "I was born an old man. And you're in a mood so I didn't say anything, but I'm glad to be able to hear now."

Okay, maaaybe she'd been blasting the music on the drive to Texas, but whatever. She was keyed up and the crew had been using the company plane for work. So she and Bradford had gone on a little road trip to see her sister in college. Cheyenne was living in the standard type of college apartment that seemed to litter the area surrounding the university—small four bedroom, small four baths, with four people living together. A quad-style dorm with a shared kitchen. The bedrooms were the size of matchboxes but it worked for college. "Sorry, I'm just worried about Cheyenne."

"I know, and it's fine," he murmured as he pulled into one of the guest spots and turned off the engine. "You want me to go in with you?"

"No... Do you mind waiting here?" She felt bad, since he'd driven most of the way. Mainly so she was free to help out in case anyone from work called and needed her help hacking via her laptop, but the phone line had been quiet the entire drive. She was glad they hadn't needed her to work, but the distraction wouldn't have been the worst thing.

"I'm good. Call or text if you need me." He leaned his seat back slightly and was already shutting his eyes.

Which was about right. The man could doze anywhere, and it was impressive.

Berlin slid out of the SUV, rolled her shoulders as she prepared to head upstairs. At least the weather was nice in March; still a chill in the air and only a few clouds dotting the big blue sky in Houston. She inhaled the crisp air and headed up.

Her sister, who was on the third floor, had called her crying last night because she was certain her boyfriend was cheating on her again. To be fair, the loser probably was.

Cheyenne was her youngest sister and had a knack for attracting losers, something Berlin was trying really hard not to focus on. According to her other sisters, Sydney and Geneva, Berlin was coddling her too much. Which...she probably was. But it was hard drawing the line between sister and parental figure considering she'd been taking care of them long before their parents had died.

She'd texted Cheyenne to tell her that she was close but hadn't heard anything. Which, again, sounded about right. After knocking on the door for the third time, it finally swung open.

Berlin blinked in surprise to see her sister with the same boyfriend she'd been crying about. He had his arm wrapped around her from behind, holding her close to his chest. And they were both out of breath.

"Oh, hey, B. I..." Cheyenne trailed off, her cheeks going pink.

But Berlin didn't need her to finish. Her sister had apparently forgotten she'd asked her to come to her rescue last night and was well into the makeup sex part of her toxic relationship cycle.

"I'm gonna go smoke." Her boyfriend, Toby something, kissed the top of Cheyenne's head before chin nodding at Berlin and moving past her.

"So you guys are back together?" Berlin tried to keep the frustration out of her voice. She really did. But she was pretty sure her face did all the talking.

Cheyenne, who looked more like their dad than the four sisters combined, rolled her eyes and motioned for Berlin to step inside. The apartment smelled like booze and sex. And a little marijuana. *Great.* Berlin glanced at the stack of dirty dishes in the sink as they moved past the kitchen into the living room.

It actually wasn't too bad for college kids. The blinds were drawn so it was dark, but the living room was neat, with a couple throw pillows and blankets on the couches and two textbooks on a side table. And there were a few pieces of makeup strewn on the coffee table, but that was it.

"Are your roommates here?"

"Nah, they're all in school right now. My classes aren't till four."

Berlin nodded and sat on one of the couches. "Does Toby have classes with you?"

"Ah...no, he's taking a break this semester."

Translation, the guy had dropped out. But Berlin simply nodded.

"So...you called me to come out here, and now you're fine?"

Cheyenne flopped down on the recliner next to her, her blonde hair cascading around her shoulders. "I forgot to let you know we were fine. Freaking sue me."

She dug deep for patience. "Or you could just apologize for letting me drive all the way over here for no reason?" What the hell was wrong with her sister?

"Fine, whatever, I'm sorry," Cheyenne huffed out. "I've been busy. I have a life, you know."

Berlin bit back the comment that wanted to burst out. She'd known it was a mistake to drop everything and drive here, so that was on her. She was old enough to know better. But Cheyenne had sounded so damn miserable last night and she was the baby. "How are classes going?"

Another casual shrug as she crossed her legs. "Good. Made the dean's list again."

That actually didn't surprise Berlin. Cheyenne was incredibly bright, at least when it came to academics. "Glad to hear it."

"Look," Cheyenne said on a long sigh, "I really am sorry I asked you to come out here. I was emotional last night and..."

And she knew her big sister would ride out to her rescue. Jesus, Berlin really was predictable.

"Next time I call and ask, just ignore me."

Nodding, Berlin stood because she was tired and just wanted to get out of here. "Okay, I will."

Cheyenne blinked, but stood with her. "Really? That's it? No lecture?"

"Nope. And I knew better. I shouldn't have come but you sounded bad..." Berlin wanted to say more, but she bit it back because she knew it would only push her sister farther away and that was the last thing she wanted. Whenever this "relationship" finally imploded, Berlin wanted her sister to know she could reach out without expecting any judgment. "You're an adult and I hope this guy makes you happy. Because you deserve someone who treats you right."

Cheyenne tucked her long hair behind one of her ears. "Now you're making me feel guilty," she muttered.

"Don't feel guilty. Look, I love you, and it's clear you don't need me." More than that, Cheyenne didn't want her here. "I drove with a friend and I don't want to keep him waiting so..." She reached for her sister, was glad when Cheyenne hugged her back.

"He's not all bad," Cheyenne whispered.

"If he was a good guy and treated you right, you wouldn't need to say that at all," Berlin said as she stepped back. "And that's not advice, just a fact. The only advice I will give you: use protection so you don't end up with a 'gift' if he cheats." *Again.* She kept that last word to herself but was pretty sure her face didn't.

Cheyenne's jaw hardened, but then the front door opened, letting in a stream of bright Texas sun as her boyfriend strode in. The guy was good-looking, Berlin would give him that. But shit like that was all superficial—and looks faded. Her sister's face was all bright and starry-eyed when the loser stepped in and Berlin knew she'd been right not to talk trash about the guy. Cheyenne would just have to figure out that stuff for herself. Or maybe just accept it, because deep down she had to know. Right? Ugh.

"I'll talk to you later," she murmured to Cheyenne, not even bothering to acknowledge the loser as she strode past him.

"So?" Bradford asked when she slid into the passenger seat a minute later.

"Just drive. Home, if you don't mind making the drive." It had been five hours here, so it'd be another five back. "Or I can."

They were back on the highway within ten minutes. "You feel like talking?"

Closing her eyes, she laid her head back against the rest. "Not really. I knew coming here was a mistake, but she sounded pitiful." She inwardly cursed herself. "My other sisters told me not to do it and I was too stubborn to listen."

"Geneva and Sydney, right? Your parents really named you guys after places you were conceived, not born?"

"Yep." Her parents had thought of themselves as "free spirits" but at the end of the day, they'd been selfish assholes half the time. Or more like seventy-five percent of the time. Berlin hadn't realized it until much later, but such was life.

Even though she said she didn't want to talk, she ended up telling Bradford about her short visit with Cheyenne.

"She's nineteen. An adult," he said when she was finished.

"I *know*." She didn't need the reminder. Especially when she was almost a decade younger than everyone she worked with.

"You need to live your life for yourself," he continued a few moments later.

She blinked, turned away from the blur of cars on the highway to look at him. "What?"

"Look, it's clearly an integral part of who you are to take care of others, but it's okay to live for yourself. To put yourself first sometimes."

She blinked again. "Did you just say integral?"

"It's from the word-of-the-day calendar you got me." He grinned, looking boyish and relaxed, a lot different than the hard exterior he normally put on for the rest of the world.

She snorted at his admission. "I put myself first all the time." She was ridiculously competitive.

"Trying to destroy people when you're gaming doesn't count." His tone was dry, and his words were as if he'd read her mind.

"Oh my god, when did you get all deep? And stay out of my head," she grumbled.

"I've got layers, baby. Always have." Now his grin was cheeky. "And whatever, it's true. You need to figure out who you are independent of being your sisters' caretaker. They're all grown now, all in college or graduated."

She hunched slightly in her seat, feeling defensive. "I don't regret anything with my sisters." After their parents had died in a white-water rafting accident, she'd gotten official custody of them despite being so young herself. Then for six years she'd done everything she could to keep them safe, and make sure they all graduated high school and got into colleges. She'd wanted them to have the stability that none of them had ever had growing up under the not-so-watchful eyes of their parents.

"Of course not. I wish I'd had someone like you to look out for me when I was growing up." There was a sort of wistfulness in his voice that punched right through her.

"That's probably the nicest thing you've ever said to me."

"Not true," he muttered as he started to pull off at the next exit.

"Buc-ee's, really?" There'd been about fifty billboards announcing the place on the drive, but she'd never been. And the logo was kind of cheesy.

"It's the best place ever."

"You make me sad."

He grinned. "That's fair, but you'll see, this isn't some typical convenience store. It's got everything."

An hour later, they were back in the SUV, fueled up, and she'd bought way too much stuff, including kettle corn, cotton candy, two pounds of fudge and a brisket sandwich bigger than her face. "I can't believe a convenience store sells this kind of food."

"It's because it's not a convenience store, it's more."

"Fine, you're right and it's amazing."

"You gonna share any of that fudge?"

"Normally I'd say no, but I bought an extra pound for you...because I know you're a pig." And because he was a good friend who'd offered to make the long drive with her.

He snickered as he reached for the bag. "Call me all the names you want as long as you feed me."

"God, men really are simple creatures."

"This is not a secret." He plucked out the fudge as they pulled up to what was supposedly the world's longest car wash, and by the time they were through it the two of them had eaten way too much.

But she felt a lot better. Well, better-ish. She was still worried about Cheyenne because that was never going to change. "Thank you for today. For...being a good friend."

"You don't ever have to thank me for that. It was nice to get out of town anyway. I kind of miss everyone."

"Me too." The majority of their crew were away on a job, and Magnolia and Ezra were on a long overdue honeymoon. Since the team was on the East Coast for this job, they'd brought in Elijah, another hacker, to work with them since he lived in North Carolina.

Which meant Berlin was backup, something she didn't care for. But Adalyn had insisted she "needed a break" and to "take some time off." *Ugh.* Instead, she was going stir-crazy worrying about her sisters, as always, and an online friend she'd gamed with for the last year.

Until he'd gone dark three weeks ago. She might not have met him in person, but she'd told him a lot about her life. And vice versa. They'd kept their names private, but she'd been more honest with him than she had with anyone in a long, long time.

Okay, ever. The anonymity of the internet had given her the freedom to be herself with him in a way she never would have in person.

"What's that look?" Bradford's voice cut through her thoughts.

Blinking, she glanced over at him. "What?"

"You look like you're contemplating something deep."

"You're not even looking at me. Or you shouldn't be when you're driving."

He just grunted.

"It's nothing. I'm just...thinking about a friend."

Now he snorted. "A male friend?"

"What does that matter? I have plenty of male friends."

"Your look is *interesting*, that's all."

"Oh my god, what's up with you today! Are you reading some psychology book or something?" Normally Tiago was the one who was all philosophical and ridiculously intrusive—and fine, the man gave great advice. But still. This was weird coming from Bradford.

"Actually, yes."

She slow blinked again. "Wait...what?"

"I'm...taking some online classes. Just a couple now because of our work schedule, but yes, I'm taking introductory psychology. Though that's not what this is about."

"That's amazing. I'm happy for you." She knew it bothered him that he didn't have a degree, though she didn't think a degree mattered for the most part. She had one but only because of scholarships. Otherwise, she wouldn't have bothered. Though to be fair, she knew she was lucky compared to a lot of people because she didn't need a degree to do what she did. She'd been hacking since she was nine.

"It's not a big deal."

"Hell yeah it is. If you ever want help studying—or for me to hack the school and change your grades—just ask."

He snort-laughed. "Noted. And you still didn't answer my question."

"Fine. An online friend of mine has gone radio silent. It's not a big deal. I was just thinking of trying to figure out if he was okay, that's all." Now she was definitely lying. Because she'd kind of already figured out who the guy was.

Chance Hendrix, aka Venom Reaper online. After they'd started hanging out in a private VR chat, she'd decided to dig a little deeper into the guy to make sure he wasn't a weirdo. Probably not cool on her part, but it was her nature.

Hopefully curiosity didn't kill the hacker.

Everything she'd found, she'd liked. And it bothered her that he'd suddenly gone silent online. Maybe it was nothing. But her gut said it was something. And she had the next week off to do whatever she wanted.

So she was going to find him and make sure he was okay. There was no rule on how she had to spend her "time off."

CHaPTer 2

The best things happen unexpectedly.

Chance slid the USB into his pocket, cursing himself as he shut down the computer. He'd planned everything perfectly, had broken into the Uptown Street Kings biker club's back office when he knew they were all out—except for two guys they'd left behind to guard the place. But they were both passed out in front of one of the TVs in the bar, a basketball game on. A nonissue.

This should have been the perfect time for him to break in undetected, but the rumble of bikes in the distance—and what he could see on the security cameras—told him otherwise. The bikers were back for whatever reason, and currently parking their rides out front. They would all trickle inside in the next five minutes and he would be screwed if he didn't get out of here.

He'd done some business with the president of the "club" a couple times, but all low-level stuff as he tried to work his way into getting closer to them. To finding out what had happened to his brother.

But Chance was supposed to be out of town, had specifically mentioned it when they'd asked him about a small job recently. Regardless, he couldn't be found in here.

Their security was shit but that wouldn't save him if they caught him in the club now. This place was closed on Fridays to everyone but members.

He eased open the office door and slipped out. As he did, the sound of male voices and laughter filled the air from the bar area. *Shit.*

Knowing he couldn't use the back door without setting off an alarm, he slipped into the women's bathroom. It was the way he'd gotten in earlier and it was the way he'd leave. He'd intentionally unlocked one of the windows a week ago in case of this moment.

As he moved to the sink, ready to hoist himself up, he heard more laughter and boots stomping down the hallway. No one should come in here, but if they did, he'd have his ass half out and half in... *Nope. Not testing fate.*

He ducked into the nearest stall that had an *out of order* sign and crouched on top of the toilet as he waited for the voices to go past.

The door swung open, followed by more laughter, this time from a woman. A man and a woman, he realized.

"I'm not even supposed to be here," the woman whispered. "It's Friday."

"No one's gonna care." A male voice... Johnny Moore. Chance mentally cataloged everything he knew about the man. About six foot even, bulky, more fat than muscle, carried two knives and two pistols almost all the time. Helped run drugs from here to Texas and wasn't too bright. Not stupid, but he was just a "soldier" who followed orders. And the guy liked sex, *a lot*, from what Chance had witnessed. As in an industrial amount of screwing. Seemed to have a different woman hanging on him every time Chance was in the bar or spying on the gang.

More laughter, then the sound of a zipper and...oh Jesus, moaning from the woman that sounded fake. Grunts from Johnny.

Just great.

"You're so wet," the guy growled just as the stall started to shake around Chance.

It would be his luck if they brought all the stalls down around him. If he got caught, he'd have to move fast, incapacitate Johnny and get out that window.

"Oh god, you're so big," the woman moaned. "I'm so close."

Chance bit back a sigh as the woman continued to moan with porn star acting chops. Suddenly the bathroom door swung open. His adrenaline spiked, all his muscles pulling taut. On instinct, he reached for his pistol even though he could take out two threats without it. But it would be more efficient than getting in hand-to-hand combat.

"Johnny, get the hell out here!"

Chance straightened, his muscles tensing. Did they know he was here? Had he missed one of the cameras? He'd worn a balaclava and gloves in case there'd been cameras he didn't know about. He wasn't going to get caught by doing something stupid.

"I'm busy!" Johnny shouted back.

"I don't give a shit. Put your dick back in your pants and get out here. Someone just set your bike on fire."

Johnny cursed, then the woman let out a surprised cry before bootsteps stomped quickly out of the bathroom.

Chance waited as the woman adjusted her clothes while muttering to herself. Then the water ran, and finally, the door opened. He peered out of the stall to be sure, and without waiting for another chance, hurried to the plain white sink, hoisted himself up and pushed open the small window.

He bit back a groan as he landed on an old Harley someone had dumped on the side of the building. He'd used it as a step to climb in but coming out was a hell of a lot worse. Twisting, he managed to land on his feet, but not before he heard—

"What the hell!" from the bathroom.

Someone had seen his escape.

Making a split-second decision, he sprinted toward the rear of the club-house—which was basically a bar and grill. Almost no one parked out back, and the small parking lot butted up to a main street on the outskirts of New Orleans. He'd have a better shot at getting over that fence than taking on a gang of enraged bikers with no backup.

He heard a shout behind him as he sprinted across the small parking lot, but he was already to the fence. Moving fast, he scaled it, and by the time he swung himself over, he spotted two bikers racing his way.

His boots slammed into the concrete of the broken sidewalk as he contemplated his next move. Traffic zoomed by in both directions, but an SUV jerked to a halt in front of him, slamming on the brakes.

He made a move for his weapon, but the window rolled down and the most gorgeous woman he'd ever seen said, "It's me, Moonlighter. Get in unless you want to get your ass beat."

He paused for a second, but rustling near the fence behind him and the familiar sound of a round being chambered spurred him into action. He yanked the passenger door open and jumped inside.

Tires screeched, the SUV jerking to life before he'd shut the door. "Moonlighter?" he rasped out as he pulled his seat belt on.

"The one and only."

"I thought you were a guy." Which was not the issue right now. But still...she had long, dark hair with bright pink highlights, ripped black jeans, and a tight black T-shirt. Her lips...Jesus, what was wrong with him? He shouldn't be focusing on her pillow-soft-looking lips, but damn. If he'd ever had a fantasy woman, she was it. What the hell was she doing here, and how had she found him? He wasn't worried that she could take him physically, but alarm slid through him that she'd found him.

"Clearly not. Did they see your face?"

"No," he muttered, about to tug off his balaclava. But he paused, since she hadn't seen his face yet.

As if she read his mind, she glanced at him, her expression dry. "I know who you are, Chance Hendrix."

Cursing to himself, he tugged it off then glanced over his shoulder. "No one's following, but I doubt that's going to last for long." And seriously, what the hell was going on? He hadn't told anyone about this. Not his former unit. *No one.*

Grinning like a feral tiger, she pulled out a small black device, then pressed the little blue button in the middle. "No one is going to follow us."

"What did you just do?"

As they pulled up to a stoplight, she tapped on the dashboard of the SUV and a screen popped up. It showed...a view of the front of the biker bar he'd just escaped. There was no sound, but the president was straddling his Harley, clearly pissed. The angle was static and it looked like it was from one of the club's own cameras.

"I hacked into the Smart Security system and now none of their bikes will recognize the matching key fobs. They won't start." And she looked absolutely smug about that.

That was...impressive. *Damn.* "Someone said something about a fire."

"Oh yeah, I set two of the bikes on fire, including one belonging to a guy named Johnny. I've been watching them for a week and he's gross. Plus, his bike is older with almost no computerized stuff for me to hack. So I improvised." Again with the smug smile that, holy shit, turned her from already gorgeous to something out of this world.

"And you're...really Moonlighter?" The guy...no, *woman* he'd been gaming with for years. Even when he'd been in the army.

"The one and only, assface." Which was what she sometimes called him when they were gaming and got mad when he beat her at something. But that wasn't proof. Still, it sounded like her.

"Okay, I have questions. Like how the hell did you know I was here? Or who I am? *Why* are you here?"

"I'm here to save you," she said as if he was the densest person she'd ever met, and glanced in the rearview mirror before taking another turn onto Lasalle Street. Then she pulled into a parking garage and kept going until they were on the top floor. She reverse-parked next to an empty Mini Cooper with tinted windows. "Come on. I'll tell you everything once we get out of here. They shouldn't have been able to follow us but I want to be careful."

Since he knew he could take her out if she ended up being a threat, he did as she said, sliding into the passenger seat of the Mini Cooper and immediately pushing the seat back. Not that it helped much. "This is a freaking clown car."

She snort-laughed and glanced over at him, her dark sunglasses unfortunately covering her eyes. "Sorry, I didn't think about your height."

"Answers. Now."

Letting out a soft sigh, she headed back the way they'd come, driving way too fast for being in a parking garage. "When you stopped gaming...I got worried. So I decided to see what was going on. And sorry, I know that's intrusive, but I'm a PI so it's basically what I do."

"A PI? Who hacks?"

"Yep, been doing that a lot longer though. And FYI, most PIs hack in one form or another or hire someone who does it for them so it's not weird."

"How long?"

"Ah...since I was nine, I guess."

He blinked, then clutched the center console when she took a sharp turn out of the garage. "Why is your avatar a giant guy?"

She paused, and even though he couldn't see her eyes, she seemed surprised. "That's why you thought I was a guy?"

"Well...yeah. And some of your stories..." He trailed off as he remembered one. About how she'd gotten revenge on some asshole who'd messed with her sister when they were kids. She'd set the guy's bike on fire, which...he'd thought had been a little nuts but also hilarious. And she'd been twelve at the time. "Yeah, I definitely assumed you were a guy."

She shrugged, then pressed the gas as the light turned green. "Fair assumption. I chose the avatar when I was fifteen and just kept it." She was quiet for a long moment, and he couldn't tell if she was going to say anything more.

Chance also knew that he shouldn't be concerned so much with the avatar, but how she'd found him. And you know, *why* she'd saved him. Because he wasn't certain he would have gotten away without her. Which was a humbling feeling for someone with his training. But he'd rushed in because he'd seen an opening and had thought the risk was worth it to find his brother.

"I was scrawny when I was a teenager and the avatar is how I felt on the inside," she finally continued. "Or how I wanted to be perceived by the world. I honestly haven't thought about it in years though. I didn't set out to make you think I was a guy or anything. It's just part of my online persona now."

He nodded slowly, finding himself believing her. It wasn't like they'd ever specifically stated their genders, but they had shared stories. Life experiences. And he'd loved gaming with her over the years. She was hilarious and a little vicious and now it turned out that she was a PI hacker who'd ridden in to save him like a white knight. Or insanely sexy queen. "Did you really...raise your sisters?"

"Yep. For their high school years anyway."

And it was clear that was all he was going to get about that. "So what's the deal? You were worried about me and...tracked me down?"

"Yeah."

"Thank you," he finally said, because screw it. "Pretty sure you saved my life." Quite literally. He might have been able to talk his way out of things, but he doubted it. And not without some bruises and busted ribs.

She shrugged as she pulled down a quiet street in an older part of New Orleans near Tulane. Older, but pricey. It was clear the neighborhood had been affected by a major storm or maybe just time. Half of it was currently being renovated. "Where are we?" he asked.

"Ah...my place. I just moved in a couple weeks ago," she murmured as she pulled into a long, skinny driveway next to a shotgun-style house painted pale purple with blue shutters. There was a little bit of yellow trim in places and a lot of greenery along the house.

"You're bringing me to your house?"

"Is there any reason I shouldn't?" She slid her sunglasses up as she turned to face him, and he was struck by the force of blue-green eyes so clear they reminded him of the waters surrounding the Bahamas.

"No." But it bothered him that she was just trusting some guy entrance to her place. He was a lot bigger than her and they only knew each other from online. Later they were going to talk about that—she needed to be smart about her physical safety.

"Okay, then. Come on. We'll talk more inside and you can clean up a little."

He glanced down at himself, winced at the ripped flannel sleeve and dried blood on his forearm. He'd felt the scrape as he pushed himself out of the bathroom window, but had ignored it. Compared to past injuries, this might as well be a paper cut.

He couldn't ignore it any longer though. Much like he couldn't ignore the dark-haired goddess who'd busted into his life out of the blue and saved his ass.

CHAPTER 3

I don't go looking for trouble, but it usually finds me.

Berlin tried not to stare too hard as Chance sat at her little kitchen island. He ran a hand over his damp, dark hair as she pulled the steaming teapot off the stovetop. And she absolutely didn't appreciate the way his forearm muscles and biceps flexed with the movement. *Nope*. Not one bit.

He was rough around the edges, with a couple visible scars: one under his right ear down under his collar line and another along his left jawline. He also had top security clearance—or at least it was still active and set to expire.

She'd known it was a risk bringing him here, letting him into her life instead of treating him like a client of Redemption Harbor Security.

But he wasn't a client. He was her friend, even if he still didn't know her real name. They'd been gaming together for years and he'd told her a lot about himself that had turned out to be true once she'd looked into the real him.

"Thank you for letting me clean up and for the clothes." He motioned to the T-shirt and jogging pants that belonged to one of the guys she worked with.

Everyone had helped her move into her little house weeks ago, and after drinking way too much, everyone had crashed here. She had no idea whose clothes they were, but that weekend had been the best. It had been so nice to have everyone here, to...not feel so alone. She shook off those thoughts as she smiled. "No problem." She pushed a mug of chamomile tea toward him.

He eyed it curiously. "I'm not really a tea drinker."

"Just try it. It's good for you." She poured herself a cup of peppermint before setting the pot back on the stove.

"Oh...it really is good." He looked surprised, and the little smile he gave her... She should not be noticing his lopsided smile. "Thank you. What is it?"

"Chamomile with a little honey."

Sitting back in the high-top chair, he shoved out a breath before taking another sip. "I have a lot of questions."

"So do I." She leaned against the countertop by her sink, directly across from him. She was glad he was sitting down, though he was still taller than her, given the high-top chair. And the fact that she hadn't been blessed in the height department.

He blinked again. "*You* do?"

"Of course. And I already told you what I was doing. I looked you up because I was worried about you. And maybe I should apologize for invading your privacy, but I wouldn't be sincere."

He blinked again and oh god, he was so adorable. In a rough, edgy way. He was only twenty-eight, but he looked older, his dark eyes filled with too much knowledge of the world.

"I found out that you just moved to New Orleans a month ago, but you're renting a place through Airbnb and didn't sell your place back home. So you're here for a reason. And you've been hanging out with gross bikers, even though you don't seem to fit in with them. So I figure you need help."

"And you want to help me?"

"Yep."

"Why?"

"Why not?" she shot back. They'd been online friends for years. That was a good enough reason for her.

His expression was faintly mistrustful. "Ah...do you go around helping random people?"

"All the time." It was part of her job.

He took a sip of his tea and broke eye contact as he looked around her kitchen.

If it had been up to her, her stuff would still be in boxes, but her friends had unpacked everything, hung up pictures, organized her kitchen, and even put together her furniture. She was so used to taking care of herself and her sisters, to always being the one in charge, that it had been surprising to have people get everything done without her having to ask.

"My brother is missing," he said into the quiet.

That got her attention. "Enzo?"

"You really did look into me," he murmured, clear mistrust in his dark eyes. Which, that was fair. She'd hacked his life. "And I don't actually know your name." He straightened as he faced her again.

"Berlin."

His eyes narrowed. "Berlin?"

"Like the city. Yep."

"I like it." He sighed again, but didn't break eye contact. She got the feeling he didn't believe her, but he continued. "My brother recently moved to New Orleans, got involved with some bikers and then fell off the radar. The last time we talked it sounded like he was going to be moving some product for them."

"Drugs?"

"I don't think so. He hates drugs. Maybe weapons, which I know isn't any better, but I can't see him running cocaine or whatever." He scrubbed a hand over his face. "Either way, 'product' isn't a good thing." He pushed up from his chair, reminding her just how tall he was. "Look, I appreciate you saving my ass back there, but there's no sense in you getting involved in this."

"Sit back down," she murmured, and to her surprise he did. Then she pulled out her phone and scrolled through to her favorite food app. "I'm going to order takeout and you're going to keep talking about your brother."

"So you're just as bossy in real life as in VR?" he asked, but didn't make a move to get up again. The rumble of his deep voice was dark and delicious, sending a shiver down her spine.

"I get shit done."

He gave her a half smile that did annoying things to her insides, so she glanced back at her phone. "Burger and fries okay?"

"Always. No pickles though."

She handed her phone to him so he could add anything else he wanted and used the moment to push for more information. "So your brother was in town and fell off the radar? Is that normal for him?"

"No...not really. He fell in with a not-so-great crowd while I was overseas." Another sigh as he slid her phone back to her. "Maybe I shouldn't have reenlisted, but I needed it."

"You have an impressive record." She completed the order, set her phone down.

"You hacked my military records too?" He was barely moving now as he watched her.

She felt her cheeks warm up. Maybe she shouldn't have said anything. "No comment." Though she hadn't been able to pull up everything. Too much had been redacted so she'd decided not to push.

"That's... You shouldn't be able to pull up my records."

She simply shrugged.

Which made him frown, but at least he continued. "We're going to go back to that, for the record. But yeah, I'm in town looking for my brother. You're right about that. And I didn't sell my place back home but...I'm thinking about it. Not that any of that matters now." He rubbed a hand over his now mostly dry hair.

"Can you give me details about when your brother went missing and exactly who he was working with? His phone number? Any burner phones?"

"You don't need to help with this."

"I know. I want to. I've got sisters and I'd do anything to protect them. He's your younger brother. I get it." And she knew that he'd lost his sister when he was seventeen. This had to be killing him.

"And you're just...helping for no reason?" Skepticism laced his deep voice.

"You might not consider me a friend, but I've had a lot of fun online with you the last couple years." She shrugged and was pretty sure the action did not come off as smooth as she'd hoped. But whatever, it was the truth. Once her sisters had all moved out, she'd been alone for the first time in years and it had been jarring. Having people online to game with had been a lifeline, and her connection with him had been authentic.

"You don't owe me anything."

"I know. But according to one of my friends, it's in my nature to help. Like a compulsion. So, are you going to go after these guys you clearly think had something to do with your brother's disappearance alone, or do you want the help of a badass hacker? Because I erased the camera recording of the pawn shop across the street from the biker club. It caught you breaking in from a weird angle. You had your balaclava on, but you might not always catch everything. I'm a good ally."

"A bossy ally," he muttered, but he wasn't arguing now

"Most definitely." She was the oldest of her sisters; it was part of who she was. When he didn't say anything else, she pushed. "Look, lay out what you've got and I'll see what I can find. It certainly can't hurt to have an extra set of eyes, and if you want to find your brother, I can be an asset. If I can't find anything, you've lost nothing."

He was silent for a long moment, watching her, but she saw the moment when he decided to trust her. At least temporarily. Then he nodded. "Okay. And thank you."

***

Chance tried not to stare too hard as Berlin did something with the information he'd given her on his brother. Just Enzo's haunts and known phone numbers. Not much, but hopefully she could do something with it.

Her fingers flew across her keyboard as she worked, then suddenly she stretched and nudged it away from her on the countertop.

They'd eaten mostly in silence, but it hadn't been awkward. At least not to him. It still felt surreal to be sitting in the kitchen of Moonlighter, a person he'd been gaming with for years. Competing with, to be more accurate. She still hadn't told him how she'd figured out who he was, but maybe he'd convince her to explain it later. If he was ever going to trust her, he had to know how she'd figured out who he was in real life.

"I'm running his face through some software programs that won't alert anyone but me if I get a hit. And the phone numbers are a dead end. At least for now. His phones are all off. So either he's destroyed them, ditched them, or simply taken out the batteries. If that's the case and he turns any one of them back on, I'll know. How did he end up working with the Uptown Street Kings?"

There was another option—someone had killed his brother and destroyed his phones. But Chance filed that away in the back of his mind, willing himself not to go down that road. Enzo was his only living family left.

As Berlin watched him, he resisted the urge to shift under her direct gaze. As a rule, people didn't intimidate him. Not after having the most sadistic drill sergeant and then later, sixty-three weeks of Green Beret training. That shit had been beaten out of him. But something about her made him want to tell her all his secrets. And that was dangerous.

If she was going to help him, he could stick to the basics, nothing more. Wasn't like any of *this* was a secret. "When I was younger, as in sixteen, I ran with a bad crew. We were involved with…petty stuff. And I was often a driver." Sometimes more. But he didn't want her to look at him with disgust so he tried to keep it as vague as possible. "My brother knew a lot of my old crew because he was always around. When I got shipped out he ended up running with them."

One of Chance's biggest regrets. He was five years older than Enzo and should have been there to look out for him. Or hell, should have just not run with that crew at all. But that had been a lifetime ago and they'd needed the money for his sister's doctor and hospital visits. But he didn't even recognize that kid he'd been.

"That's not on you."

He lifted a shoulder. It was easy to say it, but the reality was he did take responsibility for his role in getting Enzo tangled up with this gang. He'd never worked with them directly, but the people he'd grown up with had, and in his absence they'd given Enzo the push to start running shit for them.

"Is there any chance they'll suspect you of breaking into their place? Also...did you find anything good during your break-in?"

He'd been wondering if she'd ask about that. At this point, he was going to trust her. Ish. He still wasn't sure if she was who she said she was, but he was going on instinct. He pulled out the USB drive and slid it over to her. "I copied almost everything from their computer, but I'm sure some or most of it's encrypted."

She gave him one of those smug looks again as she took it, then disappeared into the back of the house. Moments later she walked out with another laptop. "I've got a program to isolate potential threats from outside sources on both laptops, but this one is better equipped," she explained as she plugged the USB in. "Also, since someone saw you running away, were you wearing clothing that can be traced back to you?"

"No, I grabbed stuff from a thrift store over in Baton Rouge. The style is nothing that I've ever worn in front of them before." He'd wanted to make sure he went far enough away that he wouldn't run into anyone he knew and he'd bought clothing that didn't look like "him." He had more than enough training on how to evade and blend in and that included covering his tracks. "Even the balaclava is from an army-navy store. Not something I owned."

"So why'd you leave the army?" she asked, apparently using that as a segue.

"You tell me."

She glanced up from the second laptop. "I honestly don't know. I pushed a little on your records, but your clearance was too high to mess with. Don't get me wrong," she added, in a slightly haughty tone his dick liked way too much, "I could have pushed harder, but there was no sense in opening myself up to being caught just because I was curious. Besides, your clearance told me a lot all by itself. Given your age, and the fact that you sort of 'disappeared' for lack of a better word for a little over a year after three years in the army, I'm guessing you're a Green Beret. Because that training is a rough sixty-three weeks. You've got no social media, and from what I can tell, your online gaming persona isn't linked to anything else."

She wasn't wrong, and he really wanted to know how the hell she'd found him. She could be working for someone he'd helped take out years ago, but if she was, then she was running a long con. Or maybe...she wasn't Moonlighter at all. Maybe this was someone else who'd taken over the Moonlighter persona and killed the real one. He kept his expression neutral as she continued.

"You have long spans where you were basically off the grid—no cell phone usage, no debit card purchases, nothing, but also no travel records—so I'm guessing you were off on various missions. How close am I?"

He just lifted a shoulder, refusing to commit to anything, but that just made her smile. And he really hated how much he liked her cheeky smile. She was still wearing the all black, skintight outfit that did everything for her curvy figure, but she'd pulled her long hair back into a high bun and all it did was show off her long, elegant neck he imagined kissing...and Jesus, when did he think in those terms?

She simply sniffed at his response, then dove back into her laptop. Again, he tried not to stare, but she was gorgeous, and the way she bit her bottom lip as she worked... *Nope.* He stood, moving away from the countertop as she worked. He casually walked around her living room, looking at her things.

If she was running a con, it was a good one. There were a lot of pictures of her with men and women, including some attractive men. He wasn't sure why he cared. For all he knew, she was gay and it was a moot point anyway. Hell, it *was* a moot point because nothing was going to happen with her.

Nothing.

"They've got surprisingly good encryption. I'm running a couple programs, but it'll be a few hours until I know anything. So you said you were going to be out of town... When do they think you're coming back?"

"Tonight or tomorrow. I was vague about it." He hadn't wanted to sound like he was sticking to a script.

"Do you feel safe going home?"

He blinked at the question, unable to remember the last time anyone had worried about him. How about never? He was a big guy, and had the best training in the world. "I'll be good." He tried to keep the amusement out of his voice.

She shrugged. "Okay, well, I'll let you know what I find."

Clearly she was telling him it was time to go. And he wasn't sure how he felt about that. "How do I get in contact with you?"

She pulled out her cell phone—with a cover that had pink coffins, vampire mouths, and little red and pink bats all over it. "Just texted you."

He felt his phone buzz in his pocket and nodded. He couldn't even be surprised that she had his cell number, not when she already knew so much about him. "I'll talk to you later, then." And he was definitely going to dig into her as soon as he got back to his rental, to see if she was who she said. He had a name and an address. Not much, but it was something to go on.

"Do you need a ride or anything?" she asked suddenly, clearly just remembering that she'd brought him here.

He shook his head as he pulled up an app. "Nah, I'm good. There's a car about five minutes from here."

Shoving her hands in her pockets, she nodded at him and he had the strangest urge to stay. Hell, he could just leave now and never look back, but his gut told him that he'd regret it. Even if she ended up being trouble, he had a feeling he wanted her brand of it.

CHAPTER 4

It's okay if you disagree with me; I can't force you to be right.

"That's all you've got on her?" Cell phone up to his ear, Chance leaned back on his couch as he eyed the street through the slightly parted curtains. He was keeping the lights in his rental place off tonight for the most part, and all the security he'd set up when he'd moved in was on. If any of the bikers tried anything, he'd have enough warning to get out of here. "She's not connected to an old enemy or anything?"

"Nope. Not that I can find. You gave me a first name and an address so you should be impressed with what I've got. She works as a PI for a security company that handles personal security for wealthy people. Their website is bare bones, but they've got a decent client list. The house you were at with her isn't under her name, it's under a corporation. If she's trying to keep her identity undercover, it makes sense. Who is this chick?" Hot Shot, aka Evander, asked.

"No one." Not true, but he wasn't going to get into the whole thing.

"Some woman you're banging?"

"Jesus, Evan, shut it."

"Oooh, Evan, is it? You like this woman."

"It's not like that."

"Then what is it like? What the hell have you been up to? Seriously, you get out and then just cut and run, act like none of us exist?"

He straightened slightly, looked away from the window. "It's not like that. I still respond to the text threads."

"Responding with GIFs is your argument?"

Chance scrubbed a hand over his face. "It's been hard since I got out, that's all. I just need time."

Evan was silent for a long moment. "That's fair. But we all miss you. We're not trying to cut you out."

"I know." If anything, his former unit reached out more than he'd expected. Every other day it seemed.

"Are you in trouble?"

"No."

"Okay, you paused."

"There was no pause. I'm just..." He didn't want to bring Evan or any of the team into any of this. They could all be shipped off at a moment's notice. And besides, this was about his brother. Something he didn't want anyone else involved in. Especially the gorgeous PI who'd barreled her way into his life. "I'm good, promise."

Evan sighed long and loud. "You're a liar, but fine. If you need anything, just reach out. We're all here. And for the record, we're getting together next month and you're invited. Nothing big, just a camping trip. Spouses and kids are invited. Bring your chick."

"She's not my...okay, fine. I'll try to be there," he lied, knowing full well he wouldn't be there. Seeing his old unit was too damn hard. In one moment, he'd had his future ripped away from him and now he was floundering. At least he had a purpose for the time being, but after he found his brother... He didn't even want to think that far ahead.

"I'll send you the details for the trip."

After they disconnected, Chance forced himself to get up. Even though he knew he should get some rest and reset after the day, he put on his headset and logged into one of his normal gaming chat rooms.

And yes, he was hoping Berlin would be there. He still wasn't sure if he trusted her, but if she was on, it might give him some insight if she was the real Moonlighter. They'd always used voice modulators—his for security reasons. He never wanted anyone to have recordings of his voice, especially with what AI could do now.

She wasn't in the chat room, which he hadn't really expected, so he logged into one of his favorite games. To his surprise, she was already logged in.

The game itself was a full-body, multiplayer game where the players battle the undead with swords and other weapons. He loved the combat aspect and it was one of the few places where he still felt like himself.

"Venom Reaper," Moonlighter said in greeting as he approached. Her avatar was a bulky swordsman that looked nothing like her. But she'd dropped the voice modulator tonight. "I was hoping you'd drop in."

"Want to hit the crown room together?"

She grinned at him. "Let's do it."

For the next hour, it was like everything else fell away. Not truly, because he was still worried about his brother, but fighting together back-to-back calmed the buzzing tension inside him. And every time she yelled "quack" for him to duck, he couldn't help but laugh. It was something she'd started years ago in lieu of telling him to get low to avoid an incoming attack. It felt like it was their thing and if he'd had doubts about her real identity as Moonlighter, they were smaller now.

Finally he said, "I'm done. I need a break." In the past, he could have gone for hours, but after busting his knee, he couldn't do full-body VR for hours and hours.

He'd healed and he could still do most things he could in the past, but he would never have the stamina he'd had before. He hit a point where he had to stop or he'd pay for it later. He'd had one too many bone fractures and ligament tears.

"Me too. I swear you're a machine," she said, panting. Not all their VR games were so active, but this particular one might as well be marketed as an aerobic workout. "So, do you believe it's me now?"

"I never said I didn't."

"Please, assface, I could read you. Okay, I actually couldn't, but I wouldn't have believed me either. Want to log into a chat room?"

"Yeah." Otherwise they were going to have to keep fighting zombies.

Moments later they were both in a familiar room with high arching stucco reaching above them, a Mediterranean blue sky peeking through the open portico and softly swaying palm trees.

Berlin, still a giant, sword-wielding man who looked like he'd stepped out of medieval times lay down on the concrete and sighed. For some reason, the sight made him laugh. Maybe it was because he knew what she really looked like.

He lay down next to her, the rug of the rental soft underneath him as he cooled down. "It's still hard to believe you want to help me for nothing."

"I get why you'd question it. People suck."

He snort-laughed.

"I think that's even more reason to help people."

"I can pay you, for the record." He'd saved everything over the years, barely touching what he made.

She looked at him, expression dry. "I'm not taking your money."

"Well you can't work for free."

"Wrong. I can do what I want."

"You're frustrating."

"I hear that a lot. But I think the word you're looking for is amazing. Incredible. Or even stupendous."

Despite the low-level worry that had been buzzing inside him the last few weeks, he found himself laughing. "Have you found anything yet?"

"No, scan's still running. I figured I'd burn off some steam and try to distract myself from...everything."

"What's everything? Your youngest sister?" They'd never given real names but she'd told him enough over the years.

"Okay, you're good. And yes, but also no. Just...never mind."

"No, don't *never mind* me. What is it?" He stretched his knee, hid a wince as he slowly shifted up to a sitting position.

"She's dating a loser, that's all. And I'm worried about her. But that's normal and I need to remind myself of that so I don't get over involved in her business. She's young and dumb and needs that time to grow."

"Were you ever young and dumb?"

She paused, resting her arm under her head as she stretched out. "Yeah, but not like her. I was dumb in other ways. Ways that could have gotten me in a lot of trouble."

He figured she meant hacking, but simply nodded. "Yeah, same. Sort of." Because he'd been stupid too, jacking cars and other shit. He didn't even recognize that kid anymore. But his world had been small back then and he hadn't been able to imagine a life outside of the shitty town he'd grown up in. And his sister had been dying; he'd wanted to give her the little comforts he could. So he'd stolen shit. And he was lucky he'd never been caught. He shouldn't have gone back to his hometown after getting out of the army, but his grandma had left him a house and... He was just making up excuses.

"So how'd you end up in your line of work?" They were alone in the chat room but he still kept things vague.

"Ah, luck more than anything. A really kickass woman saw my potential and basically told me I was working for her. Said I could help people and make a difference in the world if I wanted to. Though she wasn't really asking. She sort of bulldozed me into it."

"I don't think anyone can bulldoze you into anything you don't want to do."

She grinned at him, the big avatar looking ferocious with the smile. "True enough. I've never looked back though. I like my job."

He wanted to ask her more about her job, but knew better than to do it online.

"Hey, I've gotta run. I'm getting a call I have to take," she said with what sounded like disappointment in her voice. "But I'll reach out in the morning no matter if I find anything or not. We're going to find your brother."

"Okay." He nodded as she winked out of the chat room, then slid off his headset.

He blinked a few times to get used to the dimness of the room, wishing he was anywhere but here. Not true, he wished he was with Moonlighter.

And that his life wasn't such an epic mess.

CHAPTER 5

One day you'll understand why storms are named after people.

Chance tensed as one of his outside cameras sent him an alert, but paused when he realized it was Berlin pulling into his driveway. *What. The Hell.*

He double-checked his phone, but nope, she hadn't called or texted to let him know she was coming over. Also, he hadn't given her his address. Which clearly didn't matter to the gorgeous hacker.

He opened the front door as she reached it, tried not to drink in the sight of her. Her dark hair was down around her shoulders in thick waves and the oversized T-shirt under her jacket was cropped slightly, showing a couple inches of smooth skin, and nope, he had to stop staring. "What are you doing here?"

Her sweet hibiscus scent trailed past her as she strode into his rental carrying a giant purse. "Might have found something and figured it was better to go over this in person. Do you have coffee? I've only had a couple cups this morning."

"I haven't made any yet," he murmured, mesmerized by the sway of her ass. *Nope. No, no, no.* He shook his head and shut the door behind her.

She headed into the little kitchen so he followed, watched as she pulled her laptop out. "So—" She stopped at the rumble of multiple engines.

Shit. He pulled up the security cam feed on his phone, saw three motorcycles headed down the street. He picked up her bag, shoved it at her. "Go down the hallway and into the far room. Climb out the back window. You'll be able to get away through the neighbor's yard. There's a little gap in the fence and they don't have any dogs. Just leave, then walk down the street normally." It had been his plan if he needed to get out of here quickly.

She shoved out a sigh and did as he said without argument, hurrying out of sight. He could have gone with her, but in case something went wrong, he wanted to hang back and stop these guys if needed. Acting normal, he started a pot of coffee even as the bikes rumbled up into the driveway. When someone banged on the front door, he took his time answering it.

"What the hell?" he grumbled as he swung it open.

The president, Brody Williams, and two of his guys, including Johnny, followed in after him, scowls on their faces. All three were white and both Brody and Johnny had thick beards. The other had a scruffy mustache that looked as if it had taken him a year to grow.

"Where the hell have you been?" Brody demanded.

"What are you even doing here?" he demanded, letting the door shut behind him. "And what's got you all worked up?" He kept his tone dismissive, as if he wasn't worried about them showing up here.

"I asked a question," Brody snarled even as Chance headed back into the kitchen where the coffee was percolating.

"I've been out of town."

"Yeah, doing what?" he asked while Johnny and the other guy stood guard at the kitchen doorway, likely thinking they were blocking his escape.

But he could take these three out relatively easily. Sure, he wouldn't get the deposit on the rental back, but that was a small price to pay. "Are you under the impression that I answer to you?" He kept his tone mild but sharp. Because at the end of the day, if he ever wanted to make progress with these guys, he couldn't be a pushover. And he couldn't seem desperate.

Brody took a step forward when there was a small thump in the back of the house. *Damn it!*

"Is someone else here?" Johnny demanded, swiveling before Chance could answer.

"Who the hell are you?" Berlin's haughty voice demanded before she elbowed her way through the two bikers by the doorway.

Jesus Christ. He was going to go gray by tomorrow at this rate. What the hell was she doing?

The two guys stared at her a little too long as she strode in wearing... *What the hell?* She had on nothing but a button-down shirt with the buttons undone between her breasts, showing off a lot of cleavage. "Hey babe, who are these jerks?"

He had to hide his reaction because she had just changed everything. He couldn't kill them with her here. Well, he could, but she could get hurt. Moving quickly, he took her lead and tucked her up against him, wrapping his arm around her shoulders as she leaned into him.

"Eyes up here, asshole," Chance snapped at Johnny, who was staring at her bare thighs.

"Sorry man, just looking." He held up his palms, but Chance still wanted to bash his face in.

Brody only glanced at Berlin briefly before focusing back on Chance. "So? Where've you been?"

Berlin snorted in response. "Where do you think he's been?" She motioned down the length of her body before she went up on tiptoe, brushed her lips over his, then headed for the coffee pot.

And three sets of eyes followed her, two with too much interest. He shifted slightly so that he was standing in front of her, and it wasn't an act.

He didn't like these assholes eyeing her like she was a piece of meat. "I've been with my girl the last couple of days, and thank you for ruining our morning. Seriously, why the hell are you here?"

Brody's body language eased slightly. "Someone broke into our club."

"And?"

"We're asking around, seeing if anyone knows anything about it."

"They steal anything?"

Brody lifted a shoulder, but was still watching Chance intently. "We don't know yet."

Chance frowned. "You don't know if anything was stolen, but you roll up here clearly wanting to accuse me of something?" He made a scoffing sound, then took the mug that Berlin handed him. "Thanks, babe," he murmured.

She was acting very girlfriend-y, and even though he wished she'd left when he'd told her to and would tear into her later for it once they were both safe, she looked incredible in his shirt. He might never wash it again.

"It's not personal," Brody said, the energy rolling off him from earlier gone. "We're just checking in with everyone who hangs out at the bar who's not a member."

Chance lifted a shoulder. "Feels personal, but whatever. Check this place if you want, but this is bullshit."

Brody kept watching him, his expression hard. Then he gave an almost imperceptible nod. "Let's talk alone," he finally said, clearly wanting Berlin gone.

Berlin took the hint and picked up her own coffee, but not before brushing her mouth over his again. He shouldn't like it so much and tried not to lean into her but she tasted sweet and perfect... She was the one who pulled back and it took all his willpower not to tug her up against him. "I'll be in the shower," she murmured before stepping away.

"If you ever get sick of this guy, my name's Johnny," the asshole said as she strode past him.

"Gross." Berlin shot up her middle finger as she left, heading for Chance's room. He wasn't sure if she was actually going to shower or not, but he could breathe clearly again now that she was out of harm's way.

"How long have you been with her?" Johnny asked.

"None of your business." Chance set his mug down, crossed his arms over his chest.

Brody looked exasperated. "Lay off him, Johnny. We're here on business."

Chance lifted an eyebrow.

Brody nodded slowly. "I'm looking for some people to do some runs for me."

Runs was code for transporting drugs or weapons or whatever. Not his thing, and by doing low-level shit like that it wouldn't get him any closer to finding out where his brother was. "That doesn't sound like something I'm going to do."

Brody raised an eyebrow. "I thought you wanted a couple jobs."

"I do—I did. But I've got some other things lined up." He was walking a fine line, risking alienating the Uptown Street Kings but it was a risk he had to take.

"I said this wasn't personal." There was a definitive shift in the air now, an unsteady energy rolling off Brody, and Chance wondered if he'd pushed too hard.

Before he could respond, Berlin strode back in, now fully dressed in her ripped black pants, and cropped shirt that hung off one shoulder. Her hair was pulled back in a tight braid now and she looked...a lot more serious than she had earlier. And he liked all versions of her, but seriously, what was she doing out here again?

"I couldn't help but overhear—because I was eavesdropping. He can't do any jobs for you because he's pulling some with me."

Now Brody looked intrigued, his anger slipping away as he turned to Berlin. "What kind of job?"

"A quick swipe. Diamonds. Worth way more than whatever you're planning to pay him." She stood next to Chance, her expression almost challenging.

Chance had to actively not react.

"Too risky to do anything local," Brody said. "Especially something that big. Cops'll come sniffing around soon enough."

"Who said it was local?"

"Is that right?" Brody looked at Chance.

He simply shrugged. He had no idea where she was going with this.

"We're looking to bring in two more for our crew," she continued.

Brody looked full-on amused now as he glanced at her, then Chance. "She wear the pants in this relationship?"

Refusing to be baited, he shrugged again. "She's smart—and I don't mind a woman telling me what to do if the payoff is worth it." Even if he wondered what her endgame was.

Brody was quiet for a long moment, his expression thoughtful. "Where's the job?"

"We're not telling you that, but if you're interested, we need a good driver," Berlin answered even though he'd been looking at Chance. "Happens in three days and the take will be roughly four mil."

The room went very quiet, then Brody finally nodded at the other two. "Wait outside for me."

Johnny looked annoyed, but the other one simply turned and strode out. Once it was just the three of them, Brody sat at the kitchen table, making himself at home. "How do I know you're not a cop? Or law enforcement?"

Berlin snort-laughed. "You show up at my man's place out of the blue, but yeah, I'm a cop setting you up." Completely dismissing him, she turned to Chance. "I've got shit to do today to prep for the job, so just hit me up when you're free." When she made a move to leave, Brody held up his hands.

"Fine. If you can't tell me where the job is, I'll still need more details and I'll need to know something about you."

Expression haughty, Berlin lifted a shoulder. "I used to be based out of Miami. I worked under the name Fox while I was there. My crews were always small, we never use weapons, and no one ever gets hurt. Each job usually nets a couple mil, up to five. And we never cross any of the cartels," she added. "Look me up, you'll find out I'm not lying."

Chance wondered if she knew that the Uptown Street Kings ran drugs for one of the cartels, even if not directly. The biker gang ran some of their product, but didn't get it directly from them. No, they bought it from a middleman who distributed to various gangs or suppliers around the country.

Brody simply nodded and stood. "Why'd you bring Chance in?"

Berlin held up a hand and started ticking off fingers as she said, "One, he's trained. Two, he knows how to take orders. And three, he's got a big dick and knows how to use it."

Brody blinked, then barked out a laugh. "All right. I'll be in touch," he said, nodding at Chance as he left.

Once the rumble of motorcycles was far in the distance, Chance checked his cameras just to be sure they were all gone. "We need to get you the hell out of here."

"Why?"

He stared down at her in surprise, and okay, exasperation. She'd just thrown a wrench into everything. "Because he's going to look into you, and when he finds out that was all bullshit, he's going to come after you. And me."

"It's not bullshit. I mean, technically it is, but I have various covers that I've built up over the years. Including Fox, a sexy thief who never leaves any clues behind."

He blinked, taken aback. "Seriously?"

"Yep. She's one of my favorite IDs. I like to imagine that she wears all black skinsuits on jobs, like a sexy cat burglar."

He had no trouble imagining her wearing one. And that was way hotter than it should be. "Well, they're going to expect a real job."

"I can arrange that. We're going to get them to do this for us and then we'll use it to our advantage."

"We?"

"Yeah, we're a team now."

Chance shook his head. "No. Absolutely not." She should never have intervened like this, putting herself in their sights.

She raised an eyebrow. "Pretty sure we are."

"No. You're going to leave and I'll make something up. Or I'll just split town. But you're not getting involved any further with these psychos. I'll find my brother another way."

"I got a hit on his face. It's why I came over this morning before we were rudely interrupted."

Forgetting everything else, Chance breathed out a sigh. "What did you find?"

"I'll show you," she said before disappearing to grab her laptop. Once she set it up on the table, she pulled up a couple screens. "My program says there's a seventy-four percent chance this is him."

Chance's heart rate kicked up as he took in the side view image of a man who looked a lot like his brother. According to the date and time stamp, it was from the day he disappeared. He was at a gas station in Texas if the giant picture of the state on one of the signs was any indication. Enzo was filling up a generic-looking moving truck. And Chance recognized the ball cap his brother was wearing. "Did you get a shot of the license plate?"

"Yeah, but it's got mud smeared on it. And I also found an image of him here..." She pulled up another shot of him, this time in Baton Rouge. "Filling up gas again. After this, I can't find him anywhere. But that doesn't mean anything. If he's lying low, then there's a reason I can't find him."

"This one was three days after he fell off the grid, so that's something." It meant he was on his own at least, and not under duress. Or dead. Anything could have happened since then but at least Chance knew that Enzo had been alive and well when he'd gone off-grid.

"And I'll keep looking. Oh, I cracked open the files you stole. So far it's just records for the club, nothing that points to your brother, but you're welcome to look at everything."

He looked at her in disbelief. "You broke the encryption already?"

"Yeah, last night actually. But it was late and I didn't want to wake you up, especially since I didn't find anything worthwhile in the files."

He rubbed a hand over his face as he tried to think. "You've done a lot, and I think—"

"Don't even try to tell me that we're done. We're just getting started."

He wanted to argue with her, but...he liked working with her and she'd already proven that she could more than hold her own. But he wanted to keep her safe. Unfortunately, it seemed that even if he tried to cut and run, she wasn't taking no for an answer. "Fine, but we're not staying here. In case things go sideways we're going to hunker down at your place if you think it's safe. Or we can get a motel room or something."

"My place is good."

Even though things had gotten way out of his control, he found himself nodding. He knew he should just walk away, handle this on his own to protect her, but there was something about her that he couldn't say no to.

Didn't *want* to say no to.

CHAPTER 6

On Berlin's couch, Chance sat with his laptop, scrolling through the files that Berlin had sent to him. They'd been at her place for hours and he'd been slowly making his way through all the stuff she'd found. So far, it wasn't of interest to him, though he had a feeling it would be interesting to the Feds or local cops.

Her phone buzzed on the coffee table, the name Bradford lighting up the screen. *Bradford?* He shoved down the weird sensation he had because some guy was calling her. Jealousy? Oh, he didn't like that at all.

She came back into the living room wearing gym shorts and an oversized hoodie she'd just changed into. He tried not to stare at her bare legs and wonder what they'd feel like wrapped around him. Failed.

"Find anything good?" She plopped down on the other end of the couch and kicked her feet up on the coffee table.

"No, but your phone buzzed."

"Oh..." She made a weird face as she looked at the screen.

"Boyfriend?" he asked before he could stop himself. He didn't want the answer.

She snort-laughed, which wasn't exactly an answer. As she started to call the guy back—or he assumed that was what she was doing—Brody's name lit up his caller ID.

She set her phone down, looking at him expectantly.

He answered on the third ring, put it on speaker. "Hey."

"I looked into your girl," Brody said without preamble. "She's legit."

The band of tension around his chest eased, but didn't fully release. "I know."

"Yeah, well, now I know. She's got a solid rep. I want to talk to you guys about the job."

"All right. Talk. She's with me."

"No, in person."

The tension was back, tingling at the base of his skull. "Why?"

"Because I don't want this shit over the phone."

Chance was silent for a long moment. He needed to find his brother, and Enzo's last connection was with this gang. He hated that he still needed this asshole.

"Fine, we're in," Berlin answered for him, making him bite back a curse. "We're near Royal Street, just finished dinner. We can meet you."

"Head down to Decatur, we'll meet you at the entrance to Jackson Square." He disconnected.

"What the hell are you doing?" Chance demanded.

"What?" Berlin stood, cell phone in hand. "That's a public place, we'll be fine. And my cover ID held up, trust me."

Chance still didn't like it. But she was back in the living room in minutes, ready to go in black jeans, a black sweater and of course, black boots with little skulls on the side.

"Here," she said, tossing him her keys and then handing him a burner phone.

"What's all this?"

"I hate driving at night. I actually hate driving at all, but especially around here at night. And I need to make some calls on the way. I just want to be prepared in case they try to take our phones or something. Hide your real one and use this burner as your decoy."

"I feel like you're more than a PI," he murmured as he tucked the decoy phone in his back pocket.

Grinning, she just shrugged. But once they were in her little car, she pulled her phone out.

"Hey," she said to someone. "I just wanted to let you know I'm doing a little job right now. Not sure what time I'll be back but if anything comes up, you can track my location."

"Job? What job?" That was definitely a male voice. It was quiet in the interior of her car so Chance could hear everything.

She turned away, as if that would help. "Just helping out a friend."

"What friend? And where are you going?"

"We're headed downtown now to...meet up with some members of the Uptown Street Kings."

"What the hell, Berlin? Who is this friend and why are you meeting up with that gang? They're dangerous."

"I know that! I'm trying to help my friend find his brother."

"Then wait for me... Oh my god, did you wait to call me because you knew I was on a fishing trip and I couldn't stop you?"

Chance watched her face scrunch up in the reflection of the window as he pulled up to a stoplight.

"What? No." But the slightly higher pitch of her voice said otherwise. "Look, I've gotta go. Just keep track of my phone."

"Berlin—"

She hung up, then silenced her phone.

"So...you normally work with a team?"

"Yep. But most of them are out of town on a job, and Bradford is...just getting back from a day fishing trip. In Mississippi. He won't make it in time to help out."

"Just stating the obvious, but backup seems like a good thing," he said dryly. Who the hell was this Bradford guy to her? More than a teammate?

She shot him a dark look. "Obviously, yeah. But we've got this. And this isn't a job anyway. I'm just helping you out."

"Going out on a limb here... Are you trying to prove something to your coworkers?"

"No. Maybe. I don't know." She was silent as she looked down at her phone, responded to a couple incoming texts. "Sometimes they treat me like I can't handle shit and it's annoying."

He didn't say anything, because he wasn't sure if there was a response for that.

Sighing, she lay her head back against the headrest. "I don't want to involve them in this."

He still didn't know how to respond so he remained silent.

To his surprise, she continued. "I love the people I work with but sometimes they treat me like a little sister. They're insisting I take a vacation when they're all off on a job right now. Like they don't trust that I can look after myself on a job."

"When's the last time you took a break?"

"I can relax when I'm dead," she grumbled.

"So...never?"

"I...take breaks."

"Hmmm."

"Don't hmmm me."

He snickered, which made her laugh lightly.

"Fine," she continued. "I could probably use a vacation, but not right now. I guess I just get frustrated because Bradford would never tell anyone else in the group to wait for backup."

Yeah, he really wanted to know what exactly their relationship was. "Are you sure about that?"

"Definitely. They're all trained like you are."

"They were in the military?"

"More or less."

He'd received a follow-up text from Evan earlier in the day that Berlin worked with some former spooks, and he'd only found that out after a deep dive—and Evan had given him nothing concrete. Just rumors. "Maybe they just care about you," he murmured as he steered into a gated parking lot off Decatur, pausing so a couple dressed in matching leopard print tracksuits could move around them. Shouldn't take them long to meet up with Brody now.

"Yeah, they do. I just... Whatever, I can handle myself."

From what he'd seen, she could definitely handle herself. "If something feels off, we're leaving, okay?" he said as he put the car into park. And it wasn't really a question.

She nodded and got out with him. Immediately they were inundated by the noise and scents of the city. The parking lot was right next to a seafood restaurant and a row of shops that were all still open. Normally he liked the quiet, but the noise of New Orleans had a lively energy, one he didn't hate.

The scent of seafood and freshly baked bread filled the air despite the later hour. Combined with patchouli, rich coffee, and somehow sugar, which made him think of Carnival and king cakes, the scents were an odd combination that somehow worked for the eclectic city. The sugar was likely coming from the chocolate shop across the street.

A little Maserati zoomed out of a parking space with a woman leaning out the window, wolf-whistling at Berlin. "You're working those boots!"

"Thanks!" Berlin grinned in amusement as the car tore out of the lot, the woman whooping to herself.

He texted Brody that they were off Decatur and told him to meet them at a nearby pub. He wanted to keep things public and stay in control. Especially since Berlin was involved. She might be capable, but he was still going to protect her.

Chapter 7

Brody slid into the booth across from them, wearing different clothing than Berlin had seen him in before. The entire time she had been watching Chance—and essentially the Uptown Street Kings, Brody and his guys were almost always wearing their biker vests.

But not tonight. Instead, he'd trimmed his beard and had on a casual-looking sweater and jeans. He looked...normal enough. Which was probably the point. He didn't want to stand out. Though to be fair, in a place like New Orleans the biker vest wouldn't have made him stand out necessarily. But people might remember it more easily.

"Just you?" Chance asked, glancing around the crowded pub.

All the seats at the bar were filled and most of the booths were packed as well, but Berlin didn't recognize anyone from his gang. Music blasted from a nearby speaker that was way too loud. But it would certainly help if someone was trying to listen to their conversation—and that was why Chance had picked the booth, she realized.

"Johnny's waiting around the corner."

"What's this about?" Chance asked, slightly raising his voice over the din of laughter, music and even the televisions on the wall.

"After looking at your résumé, so to speak," he said, looking at Berlin, "we want to work with you, but starting with a tryout first."

She made a scoffing sound as she leaned back in her seat. "I don't need to try out for anyone."

"I'm not saying you do. But if we're going to trust each other, then we need to know you've got the skills you say you do. Supposedly you're good with security."

She simply nodded.

"Okay, then. We've got an easy place to hit tonight. Owner's out of town."

"Where?" she asked.

"No way. Once you agree, we'll head there, but no details until then. I still don't know if I trust you. I trust him," he said, looking at Chance. "But you're an unknown."

Berlin looked at Chance, shrugged. "It's up to you."

He paused for a very long moment, then looked at Brody. "How much is the take?" he asked.

"Not sure yet, but they're supposed to have some valuable art and jewelry."

"And the owners *definitely* are out of town?" Chance asked.

Brody nodded.

Berlin didn't like this at all, but she was more annoyed than anything. They needed to set up these guys though. Once they did that, they could use it as leverage to get them to finally talk about Enzo. She already had dirt on Johnny—so much—but he wasn't the president and didn't make the big decisions. Maybe she'd go after him later, but only as a last resort. "Okay."

Brody nodded again, looking pleased. "Let's go, then."

"Right now?" Berlin asked, hiding her surprise. Though she shouldn't be. This asshole wanted to test her so of course he was springing this on them. "I don't have any of my gear."

"We've got what you'll need."

Yeah, she really didn't like that. "This is bullshit," she said, shaking her head. "I don't need the work and we'll find someone else for our job."

"I'm not trying to screw you over. I know what kind of safe they have and have the tools to open it." After glancing around, he held out his phone, showed her a picture of the front of a safe, then a set of tools that would do the trick.

She still didn't like it, but... "Fine, but I've got to pee before I leave."

He held out a hand. "Phone."

She blinked at him. "What?"

"Give me your cell."

Rolling her eyes, she pulled out her decoy phone and slapped it in his palm before heading to the bathroom. And this was why she *always* had a backup.

Once she was in the bathroom, she waited in one of the stalls until the room cleared out. Then she called Detective Camila Flores, who was supposed to be off tonight. But she was the only person close enough to what was going on who might be able to help.

"Hey, hon, what's going on?"

"Hey," she whispered. "I'm working a job right now and can't say much. I just wanted to give you a heads-up that I might be pulled into something with the Uptown Street Kings."

"No. No, no, no. You're not doing anything with them, do you understand? They're currently being watched by the Feds and one of our local task forces for a whole mess of stuff, including murder."

"Too late. I'm in—"

"Is Adalyn with you?"

"No. Everyone's out of town on a job."

Camila cursed. "Tell me what's going on."

Berlin quickly relayed what she could, then said, "I've gotta go. I've been in the bathroom too long. I'm silencing my phone but I'm sending you a way to track me. I'll ping you if you should send the cavalry in. But don't do anything too soon."

"Damn it—"

Berlin hung up, even as she questioned her decision. But no, she had this. And it wasn't like she was going in alone. She had Chance by her side and the man was as trained as everyone else she worked with.

When she stepped out of the bathroom both Brody and Chance were waiting in the little hallway outside the restrooms.

Chance slid an arm around her, tugging her close. "You good?"

She nodded and she wrapped her arms around his waist as they made their way through the crowd of late-night revelers. A blast of cool air rushed over them as they stepped outside, and to her surprise an SUV was waiting at the curb for them. Johnny was driving and Brody slid into the passenger seat. "I'm gonna need your phone too, Chance," he said as they strapped in.

Chance handed over his cell as he said, "So it's just the four of us?"

"Yep, this is a small job."

"Now can we get some details?" Berlin asked, turning her recorder on. Her phone was tucked into a hidden pocket in her jacket and she'd done this before, was ready for it. If they patted her down, they'd feel it, but they had no reason to at this point.

"Three-story mansion in the Garden District. Owners are almost never home. It's not their main residence and they're up north this month. They've got a ton of art just waiting to be taken. Wall safe too, not sure what's in it but I'm guessing jewelry. Maybe cash."

"How do you know this info is good?" Chance asked.

Johnny snorted. "I've been banging one of the cleaning girls—"

"Enough," Brody snapped.

"How are we splitting this?" Berlin asked, because it was the first question any self-respecting thief would ask. "Because I don't work for free."

Johnny started to respond, but Brody held up a hand. "We'll see what the take is."

Yeah, that wasn't an answer, and Berlin had a feeling that these guys were going to screw them over. She squeezed Chance's leg and he squeezed her back. She hoped that meant he was on the same page.

She wanted to set these guys up, but was worried that maybe she and Chance were being set up instead.

CHapTer 8

"Hey, detective," Adalyn said, mainly just to mess with Camila.

She answered the phone as she collapsed on the seat of Redemption Harbor Security's private jet. They'd just finished a difficult job and she was ready to get home. They all were.

"Hey. Have you talked to Berlin recently?"

"Ah...not today. She's supposed to be taking a break. Why, what's up?" She straightened slightly, but smiled as her husband Rowan sat next to her.

"Just got an interesting call from her and I'm worried."

Adalyn's gut tightened as Camila mentioned a local gang that had been on their radar for a while. She knew that Berlin had been watching them the last couple weeks, but she hadn't mentioned making contact or explained what she was up to. Not fully. She'd just said she was helping a friend and had things under control, but Adalyn didn't like the sound of any of this. "We're on our way home but won't be there for a few hours." Probably closer to four. "I'll have my phone on me if you need anything."

"What's up?" Rowan asked as soon as she was off the phone.

When she was done explaining, Tiago said, "She's smart and she reached out to Camila so I'm sure she's okay."

"Maybe," Adalyn murmured.

"What do you mean maybe?"

"No, I mean she's absolutely brilliant but...I think she feels like she has to prove something to us. From a physical standpoint."

"She's been getting good at takedowns," Rowan said. He'd been training her; they all had.

"Yeah but she can't take down a bullet." And Berlin hated weapons, almost never carried them. Though she did like to blow stuff up. "And who's this friend she's helping out?" she asked, though it was rhetorical.

"Some guy, Bradford said. He just texted." This from Tiago. Another shrug. "I'm not worried about her," he said, but Adalyn heard the lie in his voice.

They were all worried about her. Yeah, Berlin was brilliant and capable—she'd kept her family together when her parents had died. She could hack almost anything. And yes, she was learning to physically defend herself. But she was one woman and couldn't go up against a biker gang. She needed backup. Hell, they all did.

Adalyn had learned to depend on her crew, to accept that depending on people wasn't a bad thing. But it had taken her a long time to get to where she was. And...Berlin was twenty-six, younger than all of them. So whatever, Adalyn was going to worry and she wouldn't apologize for it.

As the jet took off, she called Bradford, but he didn't answer. *Great.* Annoyed and keyed up, she sat back as they took to the air, wishing she was the one flying. At least then it would give her a sense of control and something to focus on. Instead, she was stuck doing nothing but waiting.

And she absolutely hated that.

CHAPTER 9

You know what would look great on you?
Cement.

"That's the place," Johnny said as he cruised down the cobblestone road. He indicated a two-story home that would probably sell on the market for about two or three million.

Berlin eyed it quietly, wishing she could pull up her cell phone and look at the specs online. "How many rooms? Exact square footage? And how are we getting in? Also, what type of security system do they have?" she added, though the little sign outside the wrought iron gate named a local company.

"Five rooms, six bathrooms, about sixty-five hundred square feet. These assholes have too much shit and we're going to help relieve them of it. It's just sitting in there for months at a time while they're up in New York in their main residence." This from Brody. "There's an entrance for staff around back, and luckily we can get to it by using the neighbor's yard. This is gonna be the easiest job you've ever pulled, promise."

"We can't park around here," Chance murmured. "There's almost no one parking off-street. Not to mention there'll be cameras we can't see. This isn't a good idea."

"Not without more recon," Berlin agreed. She didn't like this at all and it wasn't worth it to work with these guys with no control. They could be opening themselves up to being arrested and then that could potentially put Redemption Harbor Security under scrutiny. They all had to stay off the radar of cops. Plus Camila had told her these guys were being watched by the Feds. She hadn't seen anyone watching them when they'd left the bar or tailing them, but that didn't mean anything.

"It'll be fine, we've already done recon." Brody's tone was dismissive.

Berlin wasn't going to trust anyone, especially not someone on the radar of the Feds. "Fine, but drop Chance and I off separately. A group of four people strolling around at midnight is too suspicious."

"You'll be with Johnny," Brody said. "Chance is coming with me. Drop us here," he ordered Johnny as they reached the corner a block away from the target house. As he did, he tossed Chance a ball cap.

"I'm starting to get the feeling you don't trust us." Chance's voice was neutral enough, but Berlin heard the edge.

"I don't trust anyone but my guys." Brody didn't turn around, simply got out of the SUV.

"It's fine, babe," she said, leaning into their fake relationship. "I'm good." She had bear spray tucked into the back of her pants, her puffy jacket doing a good job of covering it. And she could defend herself enough to get away.

"Yeah, she'll be safe with me." Johnny's voice was taunting.

What a dumbass. Before Chance could say anything, Berlin said sweetly, "If he messes with me, I'll make sure he never walks straight again. You know I've done it before."

"I do." He kissed her briefly before he slid out, but she saw the hint of worry in his eyes before he slipped the hat on and shut the door.

"Hey asshole, give me a ball cap too," she ordered, leaning into her role of badass bitch. Which was easy, because Johnny was a loser and she didn't give a shit what he thought.

"I was just messing with him. I know you're taken." He made a left-hand turn, slowly circling around to the street behind the house they'd be hitting. There were a lot more vehicles parked along the street here so at least they'd be able to blend more. But there could still be cameras anywhere. And yeah, later she could hack into any of them, but if someone downloaded something and saved it, they could be screwed.

She snorted. "Otherwise I'd be fair game?"

"What... Hell no. I don't force myself on women if that's what you're implying." And he sounded affronted that she thought so. To be fair, she'd been watching this loser for weeks and all the women he hooked up with came to him willingly. And they didn't seem to have any complaints either. She couldn't see what anyone found attractive about him, but to each their own.

"Whatever. Ball cap. Now."

He popped the center console and handed her one so she quickly braided her hair, then tucked it up under the hat. Then she pulled out the glasses she always carried around and slid them on. Next, she tugged her mittens on.

"You're cute with glasses," Johnny said as he parked, his gaze now on her in the rearview mirror.

She simply rolled her eyes and pulled her cap down. Then as an afterthought, she pulled some of her hair out to cover her ears in case anyone was watching. The technology the Feds used could match up ears in their databases. The glasses weren't real, but they had a film on them that would screw up any facial recognition software. Glasses in general helped, but these were special.

Once they were on the sidewalk, she leaned in close to him. "I'm cute all the time. And I bite," she said in that same saccharine-sweet voice that made him flinch a little. So he wasn't completely dumb, because he must've sensed she was serious.

But...he was still dumb because now she had the SUV keys hidden away in her pocket. There was no way these two weren't trying to double-cross them. She could feel it in her bones. At least this one was distracted easily enough by a pretty face. He'd probably lose all concentration if she flashed him.

"This way," he murmured, pulling on his own ball cap.

This neighborhood was quiet enough, with big houses and walls or fences separating them. The magnolia and oak trees were plentiful, meant to give shade in the day, and at night they provided the perfect cover. For a big guy, he moved fast, sticking to the shadows. She followed after him, glancing around for cameras, seeing two in the neighbor's yard.

"Stop," she whispered.

To give him credit, he did, looking behind him. "What?"

"Three o'clock, camera next to one of the corner lights." She didn't tell him about the other one.

He avoided looking in that direction as they passed it. She did as well, but as they passed the other one, he didn't look down.

Since she was behind him, she pulled her jacket up over her face as they made their way through the neighbor's backyard. Once they were at the neighboring fence, she could see a slim opening.

"Woman I know told me about this. Says the neighbor's kids sometimes sneak over here and smoke," he whispered as they slid through.

One of the women he was screwing apparently. "What about the cameras here?"

He pointed out where they were.

"This would have been a lot easier if your boss had let me have some technology. I could disable the cameras," she muttered in annoyance, not acting. Because it *was* annoying.

"They're already turned off."

"What?" she asked as she fell in step with him, sticking to the shadows of the wall and oak trees.

"Yeah, my girl turned them off today after she finished cleaning."

Berlin wasn't going to count on some random stranger, but nodded. "Then why am I here? I'm good with tech. He should have let me do my thing," she whispered, keeping her voice low as they reached the pool and patio area.

"He wants to see how you are with the safe. We don't have a good safecracker anymore," he added.

Hmmm, interesting. And according to the Miami cover ID she'd spent years building, she could crack safes. Which was actually true, but it wasn't one of her favorite things to do.

Instead of heading for the patio, they moved toward a little brick pathway that led to what had to be a service entrance. The door opened as they reached it, Chance and Brody on the other side. She noticed that Chance wore gloves, breathed out a quiet sigh of relief at the sight. They couldn't leave any trace behind.

"Any trouble?" Brody asked.

Johnny shook his head.

Brody nodded as he shut and locked the door behind them. They were in a very organized butler's pantry that smelled faintly of lemon. Glass and ceramic cake stands lined a set of shelves, cookbooks on another, and... Oh sweet goddess, a handful of creepy ass dolls sat on another staring down at them. *Gross.* Shuddering, she turned away.

Apparently not bothered by the creepy dolls, Brody pulled out a crudely drawn sketch of the house. "The study is here and that's where the safe is.

The art that looks expensive is in this sitting room and this bedroom on the second floor."

He pulled out a small bag from under his jacket and when he did, she saw the butt of his weapon. Not that she was surprised, but now she knew for sure he was armed. "This should be what you need to crack the safe. We're going to start cutting the paintings out and rolling them up. Meet back here in ten minutes max. We're not going to be here longer than that in case someone saw us and called it in."

"How will we even know if someone did? Or what if we trip a silent alarm?" Berlin asked.

He tapped his ear once and that was when she saw the tiny earpiece. A little Bluetooth. "I'm on one of their frequencies. I'll know if someone saw us."

She nodded, pretending to be relieved. She could call Camila directly if needed, but calling 911 was out. Silently, she took the bag, nodded at Chance, then headed through the quiet house. The entire place had that faint lemon polish scent.

She was aware of Johnny trailing after her as she made her way down a long hallway to the study. She stopped at the entrance, frowned at him. "Are you following me?" she demanded, still pitching her voice low.

She could hear Chance and Brody heading up the stairs, their footfalls quiet enough, but still audible. There were little sensor lights along the hallway, lighting up along the baseboards every other step she took and she made a note to get these for her place.

Johnny shrugged. "Just following orders," he murmured, but they both paused at a slight thud.

That didn't sound as if it had come from upstairs. *Great.*

She held up a finger to her mouth and indicated that she'd be heading into one room even as he pulled out a pistol. She mouthed "No" as he headed for another closed door, but he of course ignored her.

Easing open the door of what turned out to be a bedroom, she glanced around, saw no one. But then she saw a flash of movement in the attached bathroom. She tiptoed over the hardwood floor, using the giant throw rug under the canopy bed to mute her movements, she peered around the half-open door, saw a girl in her twenties hiding in the shower. Berlin held up her finger to her mouth. Then she whispered, "Who are you?"

"I live next door," she whispered back, her voice trembling as she stared wide-eyed at Berlin. She doubted her first estimate now. This kid was *maybe* nineteen and she looked terrified. "My parents have a key. I was just going to take a bottle of wine."

"I'm here to take more than that and my crew will kill you if they see you," she said, needing the girl to be scared and stay quiet. "Stay put and don't call the cops. They're monitoring for that. We'll be out of here in ten, then you can go home." Without waiting for a response, she pulled the bathroom door shut behind her. As she did, Johnny stepped into the dim room, his pistol still in hand.

"Anything?" he asked.

Heart racing, she shook her head as she made her way to the bedroom door. She really, really hoped that girl didn't make any more noise. "Freaking bird at the window, if you can believe it. I think it was an owl, which is a bad omen," she added, hoping he'd follow her. "We should have done more recon for this."

Tucking his weapon away, he trailed after her. "We're good, I promise. My girl wouldn't lie to me."

As they slipped into the study, she said, "Are you sure about that? What if she's setting you up? You faithful to her?" He cleared his throat at that, which made her inwardly laugh. Berlin followed what the crude drawing had shown and moved to a big painting behind a massive, dark wood desk.

"Come on, help me take this down."

"We never said we'd be exclusive," Johnny said as he took the right side and helped her ease it to the ground.

Berlin snorted as they propped the painting against the wall. Then she opened the bag Brody had given her. True to his word, it had all the tools she'd need. The safe itself was fairly old, and should be easy enough to open. Had probably been in the wall for the last couple decades.

"What about you and Chance? You two exclusive?" Johnny asked.

She shrugged as she picked up the small audio tool. She didn't even need the rest of the tools for this. Not with a simple dial lock.

"See? It's hard to settle down," he muttered, talking more to himself as she slid one earpiece in, then set the other piece against the safe.

"Shh," she finally said when she realized he was still talking. She had to feel the vibrations and needed relative silence to work.

Thankfully he was quiet as she got to work, and within thirty seconds she had it open. Not bad for being so rusty.

He let out an appreciative sound as it swung open, saw the stacks of cash. She hung back as he pulled it out, then moved onto the jewelry. One clearly expensive diamond and ruby necklace and two sets of huge diamond earrings. There was also some paperwork and a couple USB drives. When Johnny went to take that stuff, she made a clucking sound.

He glanced over his shoulder at her. "What?"

"Leave the personal shit. I once knew a thief who took more than just cash and jewelry from a safe and now his body parts are weighted down in Biscayne Bay."

Johnny snorted slightly, but paused when she didn't smile back. "Seriously?"

"Yep. Someone rich lives here and it's not their only home. This is *one* of their homes. It's stupid to take anything that can link us to them. What if there's some kind of tracker on the USB?"

He blinked, but nodded and shut the safe once all the cash and jewelry was out. They dumped everything into a folded-up bag Johnny had been storing under his jacket, then met the others in the butler's pantry.

As soon as they stepped inside, Brody and Chance picked up their two rolled-up paintings. "Got everything?" Brody said to Johnny, who simply nodded.

They all left through the backyard this time, quickly making their way to the parked SUV. She resisted the urge to look back at the window of the bathroom the girl had been hiding in.

"Oh shit, the keys." Johnny patted his pants and then jacket pocket worriedly as they stopped at the back of the SUV.

Berlin snickered and tossed them to him. "That's what you get for surprising us like that." Also, she'd been planning to use it if they'd tried to double-cross them in the house. She was pretty sure that they were still going to, but at least they'd gotten out of the crime scene. Hopefully that kid had left and called the cops. Or just left and gotten to safety. Berlin wondered if she'd even say anything considering she'd been over there ready to steal wine.

Brody gave her a dark look, but she simply smirked and slid into the back seat with Chance. He looked like he wanted to say something, but simply moved in close to her as the other two got in the front seat.

Johnny was clearly driving to a predetermined destination because Brody didn't give him any instructions. But as they headed in the opposite direction of the bikers' clubhouse, she knew these guys were double-crossing them. Probably going to keep everything for themselves. During her spying on the gang, she'd found out that Brody had a couple extra bank accounts his gang didn't know about, and property in Destin, Florida no one knew about either. A nice condo right on the beach. If he lied to his own crew, he'd have no problem screwing them over.

"Where are we?" Chance asked as Johnny pulled into the parking lot of a run-down marina.

And that was when Berlin saw the weapon. Chance did too and he moved savagely fast.

He'd already unstrapped her, had shoved her to the side as he struck out at Brody, hitting him fast and hard in the throat. Then he grabbed him by the head, yanked him back against the seat as Johnny shouted in alarm, jerked the SUV to a halt in the middle of the gravelly parking lot.

Chance struck out with his elbow as Johnny leaned in, tried to help, hitting the guy right in the temple. The move was so hard, so vicious that she swore she felt it.

Johnny slumped over on the steering wheel, the horn blasting as he fell into it.

She moved quickly, jumped out and ran around to the driver's side. She dragged him out of the SUV, letting him fall on his face even as Brody still struggled against Chance.

But the fight was already over, Brody just didn't realize it. Seconds later, he was unconscious and slumped over, his face covered in blood.

"What's the plan?" she asked as Chance dragged him to the middle seat and restrained his wrists behind his back.

"I say we take Johnny over there, pump him for information. I think I can break him before I break Brody."

"I've got some dirt on Johnny that'll likely make him talk."

Chance's eyebrows lifted, but he nodded. Then he glanced around the nearly deserted parking lot. "They've got to have a boat here," he murmured more to himself than her as he started to restrain Johnny, who still hadn't moved.

Remembering something from her research on the gang, she nodded and pulled out her cell phone. "Yeah, he's got a boat he normally keeps docked in Destin. Morning Wood. Thirty-foot sailboat," she added, so he'd know the type to look for.

"Okay, you stay here with him," Chance said as he hoisted Johnny into the back, then began pulling out the rolled-up paintings. "I'm going to dump Brody and the art."

"Then I'll call it in." This would be a good bust for Camila, and even if she didn't get to claim it as her own, she'd get a favor out of this somehow. That was a win as far as Berlin was concerned.

It didn't take long for Chance to dump Brody, the art, jewelry, and cash into the cabin of the boat and for Berlin to double-check the security cameras at the marina—all fakes. Probably why Brody and Johnny had decided to take them here.

By the time they'd pulled onto a back road in the middle of nowhere, Johnny started groaning. But he was thoroughly tied up and gagged.

Pretty soon he was going to have to make a decision. Berlin just hoped he made the right one.

CHAPTER 10

Some people create their own storms then
get mad when it rains.

"I don't care what you guys do, I'm not talking," Johnny growled as Chance dragged him out of the back of the SUV.

There wasn't much light out in the chilly bayou, but at least there was a full moon and a blanket of stars illuminating them. A few familiar sounds broke through the otherwise quiet night air. An owl hooted softly in the distance as wind rustled through the trees.

Chance grunted under the guy's weight. "Jesus, lay off the beer."

"Get bent!"

"Uh-uh. Play nice or I'm dumping you right in there." Berlin pointed to the swamp behind them where water lapped gently against the marshy shore.

Chance hid a grin at her sweet tone. It was more terrifying than a threatening one and he wasn't sure why. They'd stopped at her place to grab some stuff, then Chance had driven them a couple hours northwest to an area that had once been a fish camp and place for actual camping until a tornado had come through and destroyed everything years ago. He wasn't even sure who owned the land, but no one had ever done anything with it.

He'd been here a few times with his brother and grandma when he'd been younger and it still looked the same.

"What is this dump?" Johnny rolled up onto his knees, not easy when his ankles and wrists were bound.

"Where you're going to die if you don't talk," Berlin said cheerily as she grabbed her laptop from the front seat.

The light from the SUV put Johnny under a spotlight. "What the hell do you guys want?" he demanded.

"I want to know where my brother is." Chance kept his tone neutral enough, hoped that Johnny didn't sense his desperation. Facing the bound man, he crossed his arms over his chest.

Johnny blinked in surprise. "Enzo?"

When Chance had first started doing small jobs for Brody's gang, he'd asked about Enzo—because his brother had told him he was working with them in New Orleans. Then he'd dropped off the face of the earth. They were the last people to work with his brother and he wanted to know what kind of job Enzo had been doing for them. "Yep."

Johnny shrugged, but there was a hint of something in his eyes. Fear, maybe. "How the hell should I know?"

Berlin strode up next to Chance, but he gently laid a hand on her arm before she could move closer to Johnny. Even tied up, the man could hurt her and he wasn't letting her get too close. "Show him from here."

Sighing, as if he was ridiculous, she turned her laptop around and pressed play in the middle of the screen. Moans filled the air as two naked bodies filled the small screen.

"This is only a taste of what I've got on you, and I must say, you've been a very busy boy." She made a tsking sound as she glanced down at the screen. "That's definitely you, and oh, my, is that...Brody's sister you're bending over his couch?" Now she shook her head, her expression mock-sad. "Does he know about you two? Or maybe…" She pulled up another screen, this time with another moaning woman. "What about you two?"

"Man, they'd broken up already!" But Johnny was sweating now, literally. His brow was slick as his breathing kicked up.

"I'll take that as a no, he doesn't know about you and his ex-wife. The ex-wife he's very much still in love with."

Johnny cleared his throat once, twice. "Fine, he doesn't know. And it wasn't like I planned it. It just happened."

Berlin tilted her head slightly to the side as she watched him. "That seems to be the case with you. Women just fall on your dick, huh?"

"I can't help it!"

Chance bit back a snort. God, this was better than torture, something he'd been loath to do. To be fair, he'd do whatever it took to find his brother, but he wouldn't have liked it. But Berlin had found this guy's weak spot. The woman was incredible and he loved watching her work. He couldn't help but wonder what would happen after they found Enzo. Would she…be done with him? A weird sensation settled on his chest at the thought, but he ignored it.

"Okay, well that's a load of crap," Berlin said. "I don't care who you screw. But Brody and a few of your biker gang members will. I've got more videos of you with some of their old ladies. That's what you guys call them, right? Want to watch? You've been a great source of entertainment the last couple weeks."

Okay, Chance was officially impressed. He knew she could hack stuff and called herself a PI, but this was top notch work.

"No, no, I don't want to see anything else. Just tell me what you want. I've got some money stashed away. Brody and me both sometimes skim off the top. You can have everything."

Berlin simply looked at Chance, eyebrows raised.

He nodded at her, then looked at Johnny. His instinct was to crouch down so he was at his level, but he wanted to tower over him. It wasn't like Johnny needed the reminder of who was in control, but he was getting it anyway.

"Where's Enzo? I know you know something."

When Johnny didn't respond, Berlin pulled up another video, this time of a blonde sitting on Johnny's face. "Ooh, her husband is kind of a psycho, right? Didn't he just get out of jail for manslaughter?"

"Jesus, just turn it off." Johnny shut his eyes, full-on trembling now.

Berlin kept it playing. "Not for nothing, I think you have a problem, man. You might want to get into therapy...if you survive tonight."

Chance glanced at her, eyebrows raised, and she shrugged.

"He might be a sex addict," she murmured. "He's gross but I still feel a little bad for him."

Chance shook his head. "You hear that? She feels sorry for you. But I don't. Talk, or she sends out all of these videos en masse. You'll never be able to set foot in New Orleans again. Hell, all of Louisiana. Maybe even the whole Gulf Coast."

Chance knew she wouldn't send any of the videos because it would put the women in the videos in danger with their current partners if they'd cheated. Given the way Johnny's long-sleeved shirt was damp with his stress sweat, he didn't know they were bluffing. Because Berlin had already told him she would be scrubbing the videos as soon as they had what they needed.

"Fine, fine," he rasped out, close to hyperventilating. "Enzo did a few jobs with us, then hooked up with..." He cleared his throat a couple times. "The Acton brothers. They work with the Becerra cartel."

Oooh, shit. Neither of those names were good. The Becerra cartel was small compared to some of the others, and they were going through "growing pains," aka killing anyone who got in their way. And the Acton brothers were psychos—according to what he'd heard.

Chance glanced at Berlin, saw that she recognized the cartel name too, if her grim expression was any indication.

"How'd he hook up with them?" Chance asked, focusing on Johnny again.

"Look, if I tell you, Brody'll kill me."

"If he finds out you screwed his ex and his sister, he'll kill you anyway."

Still breathing hard, Johnny nodded again, though more to himself Chance. "Look, Brody owed money to the Acton brothers, so he sort of...encouraged Enzo to go work with them. All Enzo had to do was a few runs through Texas and that was it. He was just supposed to drive their product through the state, drop it off to another driver, who'd switch vehicles...you know the deal. He was just a middleman, if that. Nothing more. I've done those kinds of runs before and they're nothing. Once he'd done a few runs, then Brody would be even and Enzo would be...made official with our gang."

So that was why Brody had lied to Chance. God, Chance wanted to shake Enzo for getting involved with these losers. But maybe if he'd been there more, if he'd been a better brother... *Damn it.* He might be angry at his brother, but he was furious with Brody. The man had thrown Enzo to the wolves to cover a debt, then when his brother disappeared, he'd just pretended as if he had no idea what happened.

"I'm going to need names of everyone Enzo was involved with and anything else you know."

Johnny nodded and started rattling off information—and Chance couldn't help but notice that Berlin was covertly recording his confession. She really was a pro.

When Johnny was done, Chance glanced at Berlin. "We good?"

"You tell me."

He nodded once, surprised by how much he liked working with her. The only people he'd ever felt at home with were the men he'd fought alongside in his unit. But this, with her...was weirdly nice. And he didn't want to dwell on it. He knew there couldn't be anything real with her, anything long-term. But...he really liked her.

"Okay, so I'm going to tell you what's going to happen next," Berlin said to Johnny. "We've got a full confession from you about what Brody did to Enzo, and a looooot of videos of you. So we're all going to walk away and never talk about this again. You can tell Brody we beat the shit out of you or tortured you for information on where your stash is, but you never cracked. If you tell him we asked about Enzo...all these videos get released. And then you get dead."

"My girl's got a mean streak," Chance added when Johnny just stared slack-jawed at Berlin. Then Chance looked over at her. "Get in the SUV. I'm going to untie him."

"Wait, you're going to leave me out here?" Johnny protested.

"Yep," Chance said as Berlin shut the back hatch. "It's a long walk to civilization, which might be a good thing for you. You need time to think about what you're going to say and it's going to be a rough hike back. It'll help sell that we roughed you up."

"I suggest that once you get back to civilization, you look into therapy," Berlin called over her shoulder as she slid into the passenger seat. "Seriously, you're just screwing everything that moves to fill a void in your chest and it's never going to happen."

"You're insane!"

"That might be true, but I'm not the one tied up near a gator-infested swamp." She gave him a pitying look before she shut the door behind her.

"I'm going to untie you now, and if you try anything stupid, she'll release those videos in a second. So don't do anything you'll regret later," Chance warned, moving in behind him.

Johnny's body vibrated with rage, but to Chance's surprise he didn't make a move once the ties were cut. So maybe he wasn't as dumb as Chance had originally thought. And he was also a little disappointed he didn't get to beat on Johnny.

After he pulled out of what had once been a gravel parking lot but was now mostly grass, Johnny visible in the rearview mirror just standing there, Chance finally allowed himself a sense of relief. "We actually got something from him."

"Of course we did. Teamwork makes the dream work."

He snort-laughed, but the tightness that had bound his chest for over a month eased a little. It wasn't great that Enzo had disappeared while working with the Acton brothers, but...it was a lead. And that was all he could ask for now.

"You think he'll come after us?"

"No." Chance shook his head. He planned to follow up with Johnny later to make sure he didn't. He wasn't simply letting the asshole go, free to come after Berlin later. "You scared the hell out of him."

"Yeah I did." She sounded proud. "You want me to drive, or are you good?"

"Nah, I'm good. I know you hate driving at night anyway. Just lean back and close your eyes." She had to be exhausted. It was a little after two thirty and they still had a couple hours back to the city.

But she just shook her head and pulled up another screen on her laptop. "No way. I'm going to start digging into the Acton brothers."

The fact that she was just jumping into this, knowing that it was a lot more dangerous than he'd originally thought... A cartel was involved. And the Acton brothers—a violent group of psychos who weren't actually brothers at all. "Thank you. But after you get any intel on them, I'm pulling the plug on all this. You're not—"

"Oh my god, Chance, just stop. I'm helping you. I know you have trust issues but—"

"No, that's not what this is about." Though to be fair, he did have trust issues. But less with her than ninety-nine percent of the rest of the world population. "The Becerra cartel is going through some restructuring which means things are violent and unstable in their world. And the Acton brothers have a reputation—and you're not getting involved with them. We're not going up against them. No way in hell. Look, I love my brother more than anything, but I'm not putting you in danger. So you can help me with intel, but that's it. And you're not going to change my mind."

"Okay," she finally said.

He blinked in surprise as he pulled onto the highway. "That's it?"

"Sure." She shrugged casually. Way too casually, but she wasn't arguing with him, so there wasn't anything he could say. Yet. Because he had a feeling this conversation wasn't over.

Not by a long shot.

CHAPTER 11

"You sure this is it?" Federal agent Anna Jenkins looked at Camila as she pulled into the quiet marina on the gulf.

God, she really hoped so. Camila had woken the woman up in the middle of the night based on an "anonymous tip" from Berlin, who would forever remain nameless. She'd called Camila on a burner phone so there was no way for the Feds to trace it back to her if they attempted to. But she knew Jenkins and her team had been watching the Uptown Street Kings for eight months and were desperate to bring one or more of them in, get them to flip on people higher up the chain.

After parking, she unzipped her parka so her weapon would be handy if necessary. Supposedly Brody Williams was "gift wrapped" for them, but she wasn't taking any chances.

Jenkins had her 9mm out and at her side as they hurried across the gravel parking lot, both scanning for any potential threats. The water was choppy, the majority of the sailboats swaying back and forth in their slips.

Camila nodded at the one Berlin had told her belonged to Brody. Morning Wood. Camila couldn't even be surprised by the douchey name of the boat.

Weapon out, Jenkins stepped onto the boat first, her boots quiet on the fiberglass. Camila moved in behind her, scanning the dock and surrounding water for anything out of place. Anyone armed.

After flipping on her flashlight, Jenkins pulled open the folding wood door to the cabin, then swept downstairs, weapon and flashlight out.

Camila moved behind her.

And blinked at what she saw.

Brody Williams was lying on his back, his wrists behind him, his knees and ankles bound and a small recorder on his chest with a scribbled note that read: *play me*. Along with a stack of cash, jewelry and art, plus another scribbled note of the address the stuff had been taken from.

He just stared at them, rage in his eyes. "Man, someone kidnapped me. Some psychos! They dumped me in here with all this stuff and said they were going to frame me. I'm being set up! You've gotta untie me."

Jenkins simply sheathed her weapon, then pressed play on the recorder.

Brody's voice came over the speaker. "These assholes have too much shit and we're going to help relieve them of it. It's just sitting in there for months at a time while they're up in New York in their main residence. There's an entrance for staff around back and luckily we can get to it by using the neighbor's yard. This is gonna be the easiest job you've ever pulled, promise."

Cursing, Brody closed his eyes in resignation and Jenkins simply smiled as if it was Christmas morning.

Camila hid a smile even as she inwardly did cartwheels. She wouldn't get the collar for this one, but she'd get credit and a handful of favors from the Feds. Everyone liked a team player and she'd just given Jenkins and her team a big win. This was going to help her career in a big way.

Even if she was a little worried about her right now, she owed Berlin big time.

CHaPTer 12

*You can change the world if you care
enough.*

Berlin poked her head out of the fridge as Chance strode into the kitchen
after doing a check of the safe house, even though she'd told him it was
clean.

"You sure this place is okay?" he asked as he sat at the kitchen table.

The house belonged to Redemption Harbor Security, and they used it as
a safe house for themselves or more often women on the run from abusive
partners. When it wasn't in use, the crew occasionally congregated over
here. Most of the neighbors assumed the place was a VRBO rental and
they liked that just fine. It kept anyone from asking questions or trying to
get to know them.

"We're good," she said around a yawn. She wanted to work, but knew
she was close to crashing. Though if he made a move...she didn't think
she'd turn him down.

"You need sleep and...I do too. Is there anything good in there, or should
we call for takeout?"

She pulled out a few boxes. "Tons of leftovers."

He blinked at the array of boxes, clearly from different restaurants. "I take it this isn't all yours."

"Nope. But it's fine. We always order extra for later. What's your preference?"

"Italian works," he said, nodding at one of the boxes.

She pulled out a bowl of butter noodles for herself while he pulled out something more substantial.

"So tell me about this 'we,'" he said as he grabbed bottles of water for them along with cutlery.

She plated their food and put his in the microwave first. "Well, I like the people I work with. They're all trained in the way I imagine you were in the army."

"All of them?"

"Except me." She lifted a shoulder, then paused when he straightened. "What is it?"

"Someone's here," he murmured, reaching for his pistol. "I hear a vehicle pulling up."

Crap, normally she'd have gotten an alert on her phone but it was charging in the other room where she'd dumped it and their bags. Before coming here, they'd stopped by his place to grab his stuff, then hers to do the same. It had been a long night—morning at this point—and all she wanted to do was sleep, then crash. "Let me check the cameras," she murmured but he was already moving to the side door. "Could be Bradford coming by."

Chance gave her a weird look, but kept his alert position by the back door.

She hurried to the other room, scooped up her half-charged phone but stopped when she heard a familiar voice.

"Who the hell are you?" Adalyn demanded.

"He's with me and everything is fine!" Berlin called out as she hurried into the kitchen, right around the time the microwave beeped.

Oh, and it wasn't just Adalyn, but *everyone*.

What. The. Hell.

"What are you guys doing here?" she asked as she made her way to the microwave. "I thought the job would go a couple more days."

"We wrapped up early." Adalyn eyed Chance, who was leaning against the countertop, watching quietly, his weapon tucked away.

"And all of you decided to come *here* instead of going home?" She looked past Adalyn to Rowan, Tiago, and Bradford. No Ezra, since he was still on his honeymoon, and damn, she missed him.

They were all eyeing Chance with suspicion and that just annoyed her. They should know her well enough that she wouldn't have brought someone here if she thought they were a threat. They should trust her at this point.

"When you didn't respond to my texts, I got worried. Then I heard from Camila that you helped her with something," Adalyn said.

Sighing, she put her plate in the microwave and set Chance's on the table. "Eat," she murmured. He had to be starving too.

To her surprise, he moved to stand next to her instead of taking the plate, almost in solidarity as he faced the others.

"Well I'm fine," she said to Adalyn and the guys. "And you can all come inside. You look menacing standing huddled like that. Everyone, this is Chance, our new client and my *friend*." Sure, she might be open to more than friendship, but now wasn't the time to think about that. She quickly introduced everyone, then pulled her plate out of the microwave a second before it beeped.

Everyone sort of mumbled greetings, but the guys were acting weird and watching Chance like he was a coiled rattlesnake. And so was Adalyn for that matter. When Berlin picked up her plate, Chance did the same and the two of them sat.

But at least everyone moved into the kitchen more naturally, sitting at the table with them.

"So what are we helping you with, Chance?" Rowan, the friendliest of all of them, asked as he sat at the table. But even he looked edgy. Instead of his normal teddy bear vibe, he looked like a mean grizzly. She wondered if Reese and Hailey knew about the crew just showing up here and made a mental note to call them. Sometimes she hated that they weren't working in the same office anymore. Or state.

"We're helping him find his brother." She had a feeling that Chance was going to be super annoyed with her for telling them, but he'd get over it. Because there was no way she'd walk away after helping him get this far. She just hoped he didn't contradict her about him being a client.

Bradford had headed for the fridge at least so he wasn't hovering, but Adalyn and Tiago sat with them too and yep, they all looked...intimidating. Or like they were *trying* to intimidate Chance.

She frowned at them, but thankfully Chance didn't seem to notice. Or maybe he just didn't care. "And we've got a good lead," she continued before anyone could respond.

"Yeah, I heard from Camila that you got tangled up with the Uptown Street Kings. Jesus, Berlin," Adalyn snapped, clearly out of patience. "You should have waited for us."

"Hey, Berlin was incredible," Chance said, nudging his plate away as he frowned at Adalyn. "She's one of the most capable people I've ever worked with, and I used to work with a lot of analysts. She's more skilled than all of them combined. Because of her, not only do we have a lead, but she acted quickly and saved a young girl's life last night."

Berlin had told him later about the girl in the bathroom, hoped she'd made it home. Camila hadn't said anything about the neighbors calling 911 so apparently the girl was keeping her mouth shut about the whole thing.

She blinked in surprise at his heated words and found herself smiling at him. "Thanks. I liked working with you too. And for the record," she said, turning to the others, "he took out two of those guys without breaking a sweat. I was never in any danger." Probably not true, but she was going to lie her face off right now. It seemed like the smarter option.

"Well, he is a former Green Beret," Adalyn said, watching him with a hard expression.

Chance went still, then looked at Berlin.

"I didn't say anything!" Frowning, she turned back to Adalyn. "How do you know about that?"

She gave Berlin a *get real* look. "I had Hailey run his information to see what we were working with. Then when she couldn't dig any deeper without setting off alarm bells, Skye made a few calls. We've got your file and it's impressive. But your brother is not. He's got a pretty long record of making bad decisions."

Berlin made another note to yell at Hailey for not just asking her about Chance. "So what if his brother has made some bad decisions?" Berlin snapped, shoving to her feet. "I thought we helped people in trouble, and I'm helping Chance whether everyone likes it or not. You guys don't own me."

Adalyn blinked in surprise and held up her palms. "I know that. We were just worried about you."

Her temper was still running hot. "Did you really think I didn't do my homework? That I don't know the things you're telling me right now? You wouldn't go behind any of the others and check up on them if they brought in a client."

"Yeah, I would." Adalyn cocked an eyebrow. "I'd ask you to run anyone I wasn't sure about—and I have."

Okay, that was actually true. *Damn it!* "Yeah, well, this is different. You're all ganging up on me right now and it's bullshit."

Adalyn cleared her throat. "No—"

"Yeah, we kind of are," Bradford murmured from the fridge where he was pulling out more food.

And that was why he was her favorite, always having her back.

"Sorry, B," he continued. "I was worried when you called me, and that's on me. I think my worry rubbed off on everyone else."

Some of her anger faded and she sniffed once. "Fine, you're forgiven. But Hailey is not," she said as she turned to Adalyn.

Adalyn winced slightly. "Don't be mad at her."

"Too late." She sniffed again. "And you know what, we're exhausted. So I'm going to finish eating, then sleep for a few hours." Berlin didn't miss the look Rowan shot Tiago, who cleared his throat.

"You know what? I'm exhausted too," Tiago said. "I'm gonna head home to Fleur and get a few hours of shut-eye. But I'm sorry, Berlin. It's not an excuse—we're just being overprotective. We know how damn capable you are. That was never in question."

A little more mollified, she nodded at him. "Thank you."

Sighing, Adalyn stood with Rowan. "We're going to head out for a few hours and give you space, but we'll be back by noon to talk about the plan going forward."

Rowan leaned over Berlin, kissed the top of her head. "I'm a dumbass sometimes, B. Sorry for getting ahead of myself."

"No arguments here," she muttered, which just made him laugh.

"Come on Bradford," Rowan said.

"Oh. Oooh. Okay, so we're all leaving," Bradford said, clearly realizing it was time to go. "I'll just bring this plate back later." He nodded at Chance once. "Nice to meet you."

Chance simply nodded back at him, watching him and the others close-ly.

It was clear Adalyn wanted to say more, but she ended up leaving with everyone else.

"Sorry about that," Berlin murmured once they were alone again.

Surprising her, Chance picked up her plate and took it to the microwave. It had gotten cold while she'd been sitting there. "Don't be sorry. They're right to be worried. I'm a stranger to them, and my brother *does* have a bad reputation."

"They should trust me," she muttered.

"Maybe it's not about trust, but just...them loving you."

She frowned at him. "How about you don't be logical and just let me be mad?"

He snort-laughed, but she could see the exhaustion creeping in around his eyes. Not that it took away from how gorgeous the man was. Jeez, tall, muscular and deadly capable was definitely her type. Just throw an adorable kitten in his arms and he'd be her kryptonite.

"I figure we've got about five hours before they're back, and I just need four to sleep."

"You sound like me," he murmured as he pulled her plate back out. "But I say we aim for five hours. Look, I want to find my brother more than anyone, but at this point we know he took off on his own. We'll be no good to him if we can't think clearly."

"You're right." Ugh, and she hated that she needed to rest. She wished she could just plug herself in and keep going.

"Two words I love to hear," he said, sliding her plate in front of her before heading back to the fridge.

"Don't get used to it."

The sound of his laugh warmed her from the inside out. She'd already liked him from their online gaming; she hadn't expected to like him in person quite so much. He was even better than she'd imagined.

Normally people disappointed her, but it was the opposite with him. And that scared her.

CHAPTER 13

Nap time is my happy hour.

Chance had double-checked the house, and Berlin had shown him all the security measures in place, but he still didn't like sleeping in a new place. Especially with the potential danger from a biker gang hanging over them. They had no idea what, if anything, Johnny or Brody had told the other members of the Uptown Street Kings.

It would be monumentally stupid of them to tell the truth, and he didn't actually think Johnny would say shit about them. But Brody might have already called his lawyer and spun a story to his gang.

Chance didn't know if Brody had put targets on Berlin and him, and he hated not knowing. Especially with her involved. The thought of anything happening to her had him seeing red.

Leaning against her bedroom door wearing little shorts and an oversized hoodie, Berlin eyed him curiously. And god she was gorgeous. She'd showered and braided her long, dark, pink-streaked hair, washed her makeup off and smelled like vanilla and something fresh. He was having far too many fantasies about her, something he needed to lock down tight. "You checked again?" she asked, her tone dry.

He lifted a shoulder even as he ordered his dick to calm down. Because this woman had him twisted up in a way he'd never experienced. In a way he'd never realized was possible. "Can't help it."

"You just want to sleep in here with me?" she asked, throwing him with the question.

He froze, until he remembered the twin beds in the room she'd chosen. "It wouldn't be weird?"

She shrugged. "Not to me, but you're tall. I get if you don't want to sleep in a Barbie bed."

He laughed, something he seemed to do a lot around her, and headed in with her. The bed would definitely be too small, but he wanted to be close to her for more reasons than he wanted to explore. "It's fine, and yes, I'd rather be in here in case anything happens...and you already moved my bag in here."

She snickered. "With all your manic checking, I kinda figured it was a foregone conclusion. Fair warning, I need a white noise machine to sleep so I hope it doesn't bother you."

"No worries, I actually listen to ASMR to get to sleep." Had for years. He could sleep without it, but it was often the only way he could actually doze without staring at the ceiling as his mind raced a thousand miles a minute.

"I tried that, but for some reason it makes me even more hyper. Will the noise machine bother you? I can just use earbuds."

"Nah. It'll be background to the ASMR." He pulled out his own earbuds. "I'm good. And you're sure the alarm is set?"

"Yes," she said on a laugh. "And it's set to blare so loud that no one would stick around if it goes off. And no rando is accidentally setting it off, trust me. Not to mention the rest of the crew gets an alert if it's triggered."

"Okay." He could rest, then. Because it wasn't himself he was worried about, but her. Yeah, she was capable, but she was still soft and untrained and... The thought of anything happening to her sent a slick of ice down his spine. Not on his watch.

She pulled the blackout drapes shut before stretching out on a twin-sized bed, and since he didn't want to get caught staring, he lay on his back on the other bed, settling in. But he didn't put his earbuds in yet.

"Thank you for your help with this mess," he said into the quiet. The white noise machine was faint, just adding a little bit of background without being overwhelming.

"I like helping. It's actually let me take my mind off my sister...and my own bullshit."

"What bullshit?"

She shoved out a sigh and turned on her side to face him, so he did the same. There was enough light streaming in from the attached bathroom that he could see her clearly.

"Maybe it's not bullshit, but I've got to let my sisters spread their wings and be more independent. I just have this compulsive need to take care of them because I'm the eldest. To take care of everything," she added in a whisper.

"Yeah, I can see that." He kept his voice pitched low as well. She was bathed in shadows but hadn't bothered with the covers, so her legs were bare. He wanted to cover her with himself, keep her warm, protected...to make her moan with pleasure as she came against his face. "Who takes care of you?"

She was silent for a long moment. "When we were growing up, my parents were sort of hippies," she said, not answering his question. "I didn't realize our lifestyle was abnormal until later. And for the record, I don't think abnormal is a bad thing. But they dragged us around the US and Europe for most of our lives under the guise of us getting a 'real world' education. And maybe they meant it." She sighed.

"But?"

"But...I ended up making sure that we all had breakfast every morning, that my sisters and I actually took necessary tests, reminded my parents when it was time for vaccinations or checkups."

He'd known she'd taken care of her sisters from conversations they'd had while gaming, but he hadn't expected this. "Jesus, how old were you when...you started taking care of them?"

"Forever really, but when I was twelve Cheyenne got really sick and my parents didn't want to take her to the hospital. My mom insisted it was just a fever. We were in Oregon at the time, staying in an RV park. I made a big stink and one of our neighbors was a traveling nurse. She called 911 when my parents wouldn't do anything. And it's a good thing she did, because it turned out she had appendicitis."

He swore softly.

"Yeah, they were a little better after that."

"I'm sorry you had to parent your own sisters. That's not fair."

"I know. And I don't regret it or anything. I just... Sometimes I wish I'd had a normal childhood. Or maybe not normal, just parents who cared more."

There was a sad note in her voice that made him want to pull her into his arms. But he knew that wasn't on the table, and that it would only complicate things anyway. "If it makes you feel better, my mom dumped me with my grandma and ran off with...I don't even know." Some random flavor of the week. After his sister Ivy had died, she'd left him and Enzo, and signed over her parental rights. At the time he hadn't understood—and he still couldn't imagine doing something like that, but she'd lost a child. It had broken her in a way he could never understand.

"Of course that doesn't make me feel better."

Yeah, that had been a stupid thing to say. God, he was not great with women. Or people in general. But he was good with Moonlighter. "I know, sorry, that was stupid. I just meant... I don't know. Families suck sometimes."

She did that snort-laugh thing as she flopped on her back. "Yeah, true enough. But I've got my sisters, and despite what you saw earlier," she said around a yawn, "I think of my crew as family."

"I definitely believe that. And the redhead thinks of you as a younger sister, in case you didn't realize it."

"Adalyn." She paused, then rolled back over to look in his direction. "You think?"

"Oh yeah. It's why she was so upset. She was worried about you."

Berlin made a *hmm* sound, then pulled her covers over her. "We're going to find your brother." Her voice was sleepy now.

"Just get some rest," he murmured, not wanting to think about his brother one way or another. Unlike Berlin, who'd looked after her sisters, he'd failed his sister years ago and now he felt like he'd failed Enzo.

It was why he had to find him, to make things right.

CHAPTER 14

Sometimes I read a text and think "what a psycho"...then I press send.

Berlin opened her eyes at an insistent buzzing...and realized her phone was going off. Blinking, she struggled to grab it off the nightstand and realized that Chance was gone. The other bed was still rumpled though and his bag was in the corner, so he wasn't truly gone.

And she hated how much that mattered.

Still blinking through her exhaustion, she glanced at the caller ID but froze when the bathroom door swung open.

Steam billowed out as Chance stepped into the room. Shirtless.

Now she blinked for a different reason entirely as she stared at the muscles and striations of his abs, then his biceps and oh, he was saying something.

"Hope I didn't wake you."

"No, my phone..." She realized that it wasn't buzzing anymore and sat up.

"I forgot to bring a shirt in with me." He gave a self-conscious grin and hurried to his bag.

And she stared like a total perv because come on, she was only human.

"You're good." She stared at his backside, which was sadly covered in jeans. Then, also sadly, he tugged a shirt over the bare expanse of his back. At least she could drool over his forearms.

She inwardly groaned. *Get it together!* she ordered herself. She never got stupid over men. Ever. In her experience, they weren't worth it. But Chance...he was different. In her absolute wildest fantasies, they might have a chance to be a couple. Or at least give it a shot. But he had his own life, was only here to find his brother. And she was helping him do that. Getting involved physically would just muddy everything up.

"Who was calling?" He started making his bed, because of course he did.

She'd noticed that at the rental, how neat and tidy his room had been. Almost as if no one had been staying there at all. She figured it was a military or former military thing because everyone she worked with was like that too.

"Oh, right. Camila...ah, Detective Flores." And Berlin definitely needed to call her back.

He did a sort of stretch-yawn thing that lifted his shirt, showing off a few inches of his tight abdomen again, and whew, okay, she could get very stupid for this man. "Can't believe it's only one. I thought I'd sleep all day. I'm going to go make us some coffee and give you some privacy to make your call."

Berlin managed a nod and *maybe* a couple of words, but she wasn't sure. Once Chance and all his testosterone were out of the room, she could breathe again. Mostly.

She called Camila, who didn't answer. But then she received a text a second later.

Can you meet for a late lunch? Wrapping up a case, want to talk. Bring Adalyn if she's free. I can be ready in an hour.

She texted back a thumbs-up, then dropped the name of a restaurant they both liked with a question mark.

And got another thumbs-up in return. *Perfect*.

She took a quick, cold shower, mostly to wake herself up. Then she dressed and made her way downstairs, with the intention of texting Adalyn on her way to meet up with Camila.

But Adalyn was already in the kitchen, with Rowan and Chance. At least they didn't look all murdery like they had hours before.

"Coffee's on," Chance murmured, and she savored his little smile as she headed to the pot.

Then buried it deep and ignored the pointed look Adalyn gave her. She would not acknowledge that look or any others. *Nope*.

"Where's everyone else?" Berlin asked as she poured herself a mug.

"Tiago is with Fleur, not sure what Bradford is doing, and we wanted to talk about the Acton brothers. I saw the shared file, read over your notes."

Ugh. She'd been hoping to hold off until she was done with her coffee. She'd decided to treat finding Chance's brother like a real job and even though she'd been annoyed with her friends last night, she wanted their help. So she'd created a file and shared it with all of them so they could read over everything and she wouldn't have to rehash quite so much. "Camila wants to meet up soon with both of us. Want to talk about it with her?"

"I don't want to involve the cops in this," Chance murmured.

"We won't," Adalyn said before Berlin could. "If anything, we'll get her take on them, but it won't be anything we haven't already learned."

Berlin nodded in agreement. "Camila is great, but...we don't share everything with her." No way. They lived their lives in the gray area, and while Camila would bend the rules when it suited her, she liked to walk the straight and narrow for the most part.

Chance breathed out a small sigh, nodded.

"So. Acton brothers. Becerra Cartel," Rowan said, his voice neutral, but his expression was grim. "Your brother is involved with them?"

"Maybe." Chance's jaw clenched tight. "I know what Johnny said, and I don't think he was lying. But I also don't know if he's right. Enzo wouldn't get involved with drugs." There was a certainty in his voice.

"But...he would steal shit?" Rowan asked.

Chance nodded, though it clearly pained him to. "Yes, he would. And has. My brother is really smart, and also really dumb at the same time. He gets bored quickly with things, has no direction...and has absolutely jacked cars before. He was moving stolen vehicles for the Uptown Street Kings. But he wouldn't knowingly transport drugs, despite what Johnny thinks."

"Even to cover Brody Williams's debt?"

It was clear that Chance wanted to say no. He paused for a long moment. "The Enzo I know wouldn't have gotten involved with that. But...maybe he did."

Berlin cleared her throat. "Listen, if we want to meet up with Camila..."

Adalyn nodded and stood. "We'll be back," she said to Rowan, clearly not inviting him either.

"I've got my phone on me," Berlin murmured to Chance. She wondered if it was a good idea, leaving him with Rowan. But out of everyone on the crew, he was probably the friendliest.

Chance simply nodded, clearly not worried.

Once they were in Adalyn's car, Adalyn spoke first. "Look, I trust you with my life. But I didn't know anything about this Chance and...I looked into him. It wasn't so much that I was checking up on you, but him. And he's clearly distracting."

"What's that mean?" She knew they wouldn't have long until they got to the restaurant, especially with Adalyn's driving.

"Are you telling me his hotness isn't *distracting*?" Adalyn shot her a sideways glance at a stoplight. "Or that you didn't sleep in the same room with him?"

Berlin blinked in surprise. "So what if he's hot? I'm hot too, and I don't distract myself."

Adalyn snickered and pulled through the four-way stop. Mardi Gras was behind them, but there were still beads hanging in most of the trees they drove under. Though that was pretty much a guarantee year-round at this point.

"Does Rowan distract you?"

"Hell yeah he does, all the time," Adalyn murmured. "The man is a giant, walking distraction."

The tension in Berlin's chest eased. "It felt like you were checking up on me in a way you wouldn't with the guys. That's what bothered me so much."

Adalyn nodded slightly. "I was, but not how you think. The world is cruel to women and it's a hell of lot more violent to us. So yeah, I worry about you in ways I don't worry about the guys. And that's not changing, because reality sucks. So I'm not sorry for checking up on you, but I'm sorry if I made you feel less than or less capable. Because I don't see you like that. You're one of the smartest, most terrifying people I know."

The praise warmed her insides. "That's the nicest thing you've ever said to me."

She lifted a shoulder. "It's true. And I'm going to worry about you. So get used to it."

Berlin's throat tightened with unexpected emotion. And she recognized the irony of her being worried about her sisters all the time, and then getting annoyed when Adalyn was worried about her. It was...nice to have someone concerned about her. "Okay."

Adalyn nodded once and the conversation was done as she pulled into a parking spot at the little hole-in-the-wall Indian place they loved. "So what's the plan with Camila?"

Berlin shrugged. "I don't know—she contacted me. I say we just find out everything we can and fish around about the Acton brothers. Maybe she knows something about them we haven't found yet."

On the same page, they headed inside and found Camila was already seated in a booth facing the door, a glass of water in front of her. She had on jeans and a simple black sweater, her dark hair pulled up into a ponytail, and simple gold hoops in her ears. Her badge wasn't anywhere to be seen so Berlin assumed she was off the clock or keeping it tucked away for lunch.

Adalyn sat on the same side with Camila—no doubt because she wanted eyes on the door too—and Berlin sat on the opposite side. She trusted them both to have her back. "Have you been waiting long?"

"Nah, just got here. Thanks for meeting me. Oh, are you going to Magnolia's tonight?"

Berlin looked at Adalyn, eyebrows raised.

"Oh right, they just got back from their honeymoon, wanted to have everyone over. You're invited," Adalyn said to Berlin. "I forgot to tell you."

Berlin didn't commit one way or another, because she wasn't sure if that was an option tonight. Anything could happen with Chance at this point.

"Mari's gonna be there," Camila added.

"I'll be there," she said, because she adored the other woman. A corporate pilot who owned multiple small airports around the US, she had her shit together in a way Berlin only aspired to. When she wanted something, she went for it, and Berlin flat-out admired her ability to not give a shit what anyone thought.

"So, what's the deal?" Adalyn asked.

"Can a girl order some food first?" Camila's tone was dry, but she grinned. "And I've got good news." She trailed off as their server approached, took their drink and appetizer order. Then she said, "Brody

Williams is going away for a few years, but he cut a deal. He's flipping on some other guys. And while it's helping the Feds, I think he should have just done his time. They'll find out he snitched and someone will go after him. But that's not my problem." She shrugged.

"Any news on Johnny Moore?" Berlin asked.

She shook her head. "Nothing yet."

Yeah, Berlin hadn't gotten a hit on the guy's face in any of her software, or seen that he'd used his credit card anywhere. So maybe he was still walking home. Or maybe he'd gotten eaten by gators. She nearly snorted at the thought. As she was trying to think of a subtle way to ask about the Acton brothers and what Camila knew, Camila continued.

"So, we also got a weird call from the neighbor of the place you guys were at last night." Camila kept her words vague enough. "She said she saw someone breaking into the place, but when a detective spoke to her, she was a little hesitant to sign her statement."

Berlin snorted softly. "Yeah, because she was inside the house at the time."

Camila's dark eyes widened. "What?"

"Yep." She quickly recapped everything, which made Camila shake her head.

"God, kids are dumb sometimes. And I know nineteen isn't a kid exactly, but..."

Adalyn laughed. "It totally is."

Camila cleared her throat, her expression shifting. "So this isn't work related but...friend related. I need advice. I'm going to talk to Magnolia but I wanted your advice too, and she's too close to the situation, I think. I found out that Emma's mom died. She knows and says she's fine, but I know that can't be true."

Berlin nodded quietly. Emma was a teenage girl Camila had taken in so she'd have some stability for her senior year of high school when her mom had bailed. Before that she'd been couch surfing with friends and lying about where her mom was. Since Emma was dating Lucas, Magnolia and Ezra's son, Camila was right—Magnolia might be too close to any situation involving her.

"I've offered to get her therapy, which she says she'll think about." Camila let out a long breath. "I know she's almost eighteen and I never saw myself in this kind of situation, but we'd talked about me officially adopting her once she was old enough to legally make the decision for herself. But now..."

"Now you're worried that if you bring it up again, it'll sound callous."

"Yeah." Camila nodded, then they were all quiet as their server delivered their plates. Once they were alone again, she continued. "I don't even know what I'm asking. I'm just...struggling, I guess. And it doesn't help that I barely see her because she's involved in a new play. Or with Lucas." Her tone was dry, but she smiled with pure parental affection.

"Just talk to her," Berlin said. "Let her know that you haven't changed your mind and you'll always be there for her no matter what she decides to do."

"You're right. I know that. It's just finding the words." She sighed. "Ugh, jumping into this parenthood thing with an almost fully grown person was supposed to be easier."

Now Berlin snickered. "I don't think it's ever easy." She'd been the guardian of her three sisters when they'd all been teens and it had been...a lot. But she didn't want to think about that now.

After they'd eaten and caught up on other things, Camila said, "So what else do you guys want to know?"

"What makes you think we have anything else to ask?" Adalyn asked.

"Because I know you both. And there has to be a reason you," she said, looking at Berlin now, "were working with those two lowlifes. And Williams didn't mention you, by the way."

"Really?"

"He didn't say a word about you or your partner, who I want to meet," she added.

Berlin hadn't given Camila much about Chance, not even his name. She'd just told the detective that he was her friend and she was helping him find his brother. "That's interesting."

"Yeah, he's not mentioning him or you because he's likely planning to get revenge later."

"It's not like he knows my real identity."

"Does he know your friend? *His* real identity?"

"Yeah, he knows my friend."

"Well that's something to think about, then."

Berlin had already thought of that, and Chance was aware that Williams might come after him later. "I know, thank you."

"And you're right, we've got some questions about the Acton brothers."

Camila looked up from her tikka masala, blinked once. "You know who they are, right?"

"Yep." Adalyn's voice was neutral enough, but Berlin knew she hated this. To be fair, they'd tangled with way worse people than the Acton brothers. And she was going to find Chance's brother, with or without their help.

"Okay...they're violent psychopaths, to put it bluntly." Camila kept her voice low as she glanced around, but the place was busy and no one was paying attention to them. "They're on a federal watchlist and for a while it was suspected they had a small place here they used as a bolt-hole. Are you saying they're in bed with the Uptown Street Kings?"

Berlin glanced at Adalyn, then looked back at Camila and nodded. "It sounds like it. I think the gang, or maybe Williams personally, owed them a debt."

Camila made a face. "I can only imagine how costly that would be. They kill entire families if you cross them. The Feds have already taken Williams into their custody, but I'll tell them to push that angle. Maybe they'll get something useful."

"Thanks," Berlin said. It was all they could ask for. Because there wasn't much of a connection between Williams—that Berlin could find anyway—and the Acton brothers. And she hated to admit it, but there wasn't much she'd found on them at all so far.

She'd done her normal searches, but these guys were ghosts. They did dirty work for the Becerra cartel in the US mostly. They moved product from Arizona all the way to the East Coast. And they used different people or gangs not affiliated with them or the cartel to do it. Through debts, fear, or in exchange for cash. They liked to outsource, it seemed. Which was really smart.

But it sucked for Berlin because she and her crew were stuck at square one until they could locate the psychos.

CHaPTer 15

"What are you doing out here?" Mari slid onto the bench next to her, glass of white wine in hand. Mari was petite with long, dark hair that was almost blue-black in the right light.

Berlin had come over to Ezra and Magnolia's to see them after their honeymoon, but she'd stepped outside because she was expecting a phone call and wanted privacy when she answered. Currently everyone was in their huge kitchen chatting, drinking and eating all the delicious snacks set out. Chance was back at the safe house and Berlin could admit she wished she was there with him. "Just waiting on a call."

"Liar." Mari polished off her drink, then set the glass down.

"I'm serious. It's work." She really was waiting for a call from someone she hadn't wanted to bother, but at this point she was out of moves. "But I don't want to talk about work. What's going on with you? I haven't seen you since the wedding."

"Honestly, just work. Then more work. I need a freaking vacation." Sighing, Mari lay her head on Berlin's shoulder as they both looked out at the glittering pool. "Somewhere cold."

"Cold?" Berlin stretched her feet out on the table next to Mari. Even though they hadn't known each other that long, Berlin could be herself with the other woman. "Don't people usually like to go somewhere warm, with sand?"

"Ugh. Sand. It gets in everything."

Berlin snickered.

"I want to go to the mountains and hole up in front of a fireplace or firepit with hot cocoa, a good book, and just turn off my brain for a week."

"Anything particular going on at work?" Because she knew Mari loved her job as a corporate pilot, among other ventures.

"No...maybe, but I don't want to talk about it either."

"That's fair." She paused, sighed. "I went to see Cheyenne when she was upset over her cheating boyfriend, and now she's back with the loser."

"Ugh. I'm sorry. That really sucks."

"Yeah, it does." Berlin loved how Mari simply listened and rarely offered advice unless asked. Listening was a skill, and Berlin tried to emulate her friend, but it was hard, especially being the oldest of four. She was a fixer and wanted to help when she could. "I shouldn't have gone to see her. I should have just let her vent to me and then left it alone."

"Yeah, probably. But...you're a good big sister. Meanwhile, my brothers are assfaces."

"Okay, now who's the liar. You love your brothers."

Raising her head, Mari grinned. "True, but they're my brothers so I've gotta give them grief."

Berlin's phone buzzed in her lap and her heart rate kicked up.

"Oh, I know that look. Work. I'll be inside." Mari picked up her empty glass and disappeared as Berlin answered.

"Hazel, hey, I'm really sorry to bother you, but thanks for calling me back." Special Agent Hazel Blake worked for the FBI and was friends with Skye and Leighton, two of the founders of Redemption Harbor Security.

She'd also been a Cobra pilot in the Air Force years before. Berlin really admired the other woman, and for the most part almost never involved her in any of their jobs. She knew that Skye and Hailey occasionally called her for intel, but Berlin never wanted to push their relationship. She wasn't friends with her the way the others were.

"It's no problem at all. And I looked into that thing you told me about... I don't work with the task force that handles that particular group. That task force works with the DEA, and from what I hear, they've had a leak for a while and can't seem to plug it."

"So what does that mean?"

"It means the information on the 'brothers' is scant. And anything that comes in usually amounts to nothing."

Disappointment slid through Berlin at her words. "Well, thank you for looking into them anyway. I really appreciate it." *Damn, another dead end. Now what?*

"I'm not done," Hazel said, and Berlin swore she could hear a smile in her voice. "I might have a way for you to get closer to them. The people they work with use different modes of transportation for their product, including speedboats through Louisiana. Honestly, their system is incredibly well organized and better than most legit businesses. Unfortunately for us they keep the separate parts of it insulated. Anyway, they work with a couple different outfits in your state, one you already know about. But they also work with the Backwater Bayou Boys—and I can't believe that's their name," she muttered. "They transport anything and everything for them through the swamps. No one's been able to nail them down, but I have new details on when the Boys will be making a run. This Tuesday, so you've got a day and some change to plan something. One of their members was picked up and agreed to turn state's evidence. I think we can turn more of their gang."

"If you could jeopardize your job, don't tell me anything more." Because this was more than gray area now.

"I've thought this over, and my contact with the task force, my friend...they okayed me reaching out to you. Not you personally or your company, but they're frustrated about the mole and want something done. If you can get someone from the Backwater Bayou Boys to give you more info on the Acton brothers, then do it. But I expect you to share that information. I'll treat any information from you as if I got it from a CI."

"Absolutely. Thank you."

"I'm going to upload what I've got. Unless you want it a different way?"

Hazel had sent information in the past to a secure folder Berlin had earmarked for intel from outside sources. And if there were ever too many brute force attacks on it in the hopes of hacking it, she'd set it to destroy itself. "Nope, that's perfect. Thank you again."

"Keep me updated."

Once they disconnected, adrenaline punched through Berlin. This might amount to nothing, but it was a start. Sometimes cases were all about following the next lead, to the next lead, to hopefully what they needed in the first place. Not all cases were like this—normally they had a lot more to go on. But she wasn't going to sleep on this lead.

Instead of heading back inside, she snuck out through the back gate and made her way to her car. Once she was inside, she texted the others letting them know she'd had to run.

They'd probably be annoyed but it was easier to duck out this way and get started digging. And okay, she wanted to get back to Chance.

He was at the safe house and likely going out of his mind without anything to do. She knew he wanted to be out there doing something to find his brother. Hopefully now they were one step closer.

She also hoped to get over this growing crush, because she couldn't stop fantasizing about Chance. And she knew if she acted on it, it would end in disaster. Too much was on the line right now.

CHAPTER 16

*I've learned so much from my mistakes that
I'm thinking of making a few more.*

Chance glanced up as Berlin stepped into the safe house kitchen, smiled and mouthed *almost done* to her as he said, "Thanks for answering. Just let me know if you hear anything." Sighing, he set the phone down as she locked the door behind her.

"Everything okay?"

"Yeah, just reaching out to people I've already talked to about Enzo. I was hoping maybe he came home or something." Chance had known it was a shot in the dark, but had wanted to be doing something instead of just sitting around and waiting. His brother's phone was off, and Berlin couldn't find any online movement from him.

"By your expression, no luck?"

He shook his head. "How was dinner?" She'd asked him to go, but it had been clear the people she worked with didn't want him there so he'd hung back. These weren't his friends. Except for Berlin.

"It was good to see Ezra and Magnolia. And I might have a lead. Don't get too excited but the Backwater Bayou Boys out of Baton Rouge might be running what I assume is drugs this Tuesday—and I'm going to be calling them the Boys from this point forward because their name is so stupid. Anyway, a friend sent me some information about them and they're potentially linked to the Acton brothers. I can't actually show the information to you, but once I've read over everything I'll let you know what I've got. Then we can decide on a plan."

"What does your crew think of this?"

"Ah, they don't even know yet. I didn't tell them." She grinned mischievously and he felt that look like a punch to his chest. God, she was gorgeous and so smart it hurt his brain a little. "I texted them once I'd already left the party. Things were winding down anyway and this way I didn't have to do goodbyes."

"Or get questioned about where you got your intel?" he asked dryly.

She blinked in surprise, then grinned again. "It's like you're in my head."

He just shrugged, but he was glad she wasn't in *his* head. Because he couldn't stop thinking about her—and it had nothing to do with her helping him. Nothing to do with finding his brother. And everything to do with his growing fascination with her. Hell, he wasn't just thinking about her, he was obsessed with the woman.

He'd always had fun with Moonlighter online, had acted like he did with his old unit. Because he'd assumed she was a man. Then last night—or this morning technically—they'd shared a room. Which should have been weird, but it strangely wasn't. He'd always been himself with her, and now that they'd met in person it was no different. Except everything was different. "Is there anything I can do to help?"

"I wish, but no. I'm going to hang out in the living room and work. There's a VR set in there you can use if you want. I'm the only one who ever uses it. It's my backup."

"I actually brought mine. Would you mind if I worked out a little? I don't want to distract you," he added as he followed her into the expansive room. The safe house itself was huge, but warm and inviting. There were throw blankets in a basket by a fireplace, a big television above it and comfortable couches.

"Of course not, go for it. I'd rather not be alone anyway. Normally I've got a full house when I'm working, or someone in my ear asking for information."

He laughed lightly at her description as she stretched out on one of the couches, her laptop open. He was pretty sure he ceased to exist for her then as she focused on her screen.

As she worked, he started simple calisthenics: pushups and crunches until he had to strip off his shirt. He'd have preferred to go for a long run, but even with Brody Williams in custody, they still weren't sure where Johnny was. He wondered if leaving the guy like that had been a mistake, but it had been the only real option. So Chance was trying to do the smart thing and stick to the safe house, even though he was already going out of his mind. Though being cooped up with Berlin wasn't a bad thing. Except he couldn't stop fantasizing about her, wondering if she'd welcome him into her bed tonight.

After so many crunches he'd lost count, he glanced over to find her watching him with...interest.

Flushing slightly, she quickly glanced back at her screen. Her dark hair was pulled up into a loose ponytail, with little tendrils down around her face.

"Am I bothering you?" he asked, wondering if he was seeing what he wanted or if she'd been watching him the same way he watched her when she wasn't paying attention.

"No, I'm just impressed by how many sit-ups you did," she rasped out, her voice unsteady.

"I work out when I'm stressed." Or when he was bored. Or...all the time really. It had been a way for him to cope with shit growing up. He hadn't been able to do anything for his sister, hadn't been able to afford the treatment she'd needed. He'd had no control over anything except himself.

Then the army had only fed that need for him to stay in shape. A few years in, he'd discovered VR, another one of his coping mechanisms. And if he was being honest, he tried to keep his body honed because of his knee. He had a need to stay strong everywhere in case part of his body betrayed him again.

"I wish I had your stamina." She paused, then cleared her throat and ducked her head a little as she continued working, her cheeks even pinker now.

He couldn't help but grin as he rolled over, started on another round of pushups now. "You hold your own when we're gaming."

She snickered slightly. "True. That's because I'm competitive though. I hate losing anything."

Maybe she didn't run or do weights, but she was lean and had kicked his ass on more than one occasion during their games. As he continued working out, she was clearly making progress on her laptop. But eventually his knee started to bother him.

"You okay?" Berlin's voice cut through his thoughts.

"What?"

"You winced slightly." She rolled her neck as she slid her laptop off her lap and stood. "Is it your knee?"

He'd told her about his knee before he'd known who she really was, and while he hadn't been able to tell her all the details, he'd been honest enough about the pain. "Yeah." Hiding another wince, he sat up and started stretching his leg slowly. "Some days it's fine and others... Whatever, it's okay."

She gave him a dubious look but didn't push him, thankfully.

"It's not fine actually. It sucks some days," he finally said. "It's why I got out of the army. I could have stayed in, but not with my unit. And things wouldn't have ever been the same. So I opted to end my contract. It...would have been too painful to stay in. And now I have no idea what I'm doing with my life other than trying to find my brother."

She sat on the ground across from him. "I'm really sorry. That does suck."

He shoved out a breath, surprised by how honest he'd been with her. The last part he hadn't said aloud to anyone, had barely let himself acknowledge how much he was drifting. "I keep pushing my unit away. Or maybe not, but I'm not 'engaging' with them like I used to. Not my word." His friends had all been reaching out, especially Hot Shot. Deep down he kept wondering when they'd all forget about him and move on.

"It's got to be hard knowing they're out there doing what you used to do, without you."

"Yeah, it is." This close to her, he could drown in her blue-green eyes, and god, he told himself *not* to want her. But that was like telling the sun not to shine. He cleared his throat as he looked away, using stretching as an excuse to break eye contact. "Find anything good?"

"Maybe." She flopped down next to him on the throw rug, propped her hands under her head. "These 'Boys,' aka assholes, run drugs using airboats through some pretty complex river systems. It's an expansive area, but...I hacked into a satellite and found some old images we might be able to use to pinpoint which rivers they're using. It's a long shot, but it's something. I need to talk to the others, see what they think we should do."

"You hacked a satellite?"

"Yeah. A decommissioned one." She shrugged, like it was no big deal, but then she smiled.

"You know how amazing that is."

"I do." Now her grin was a little terrifying.

"I feel like you could take over some small governments if you wanted."

"The thought has crossed my mind." Laughing lightly, she sat up just as he started to move, putting them a lot closer together than they had been before.

Her sweet hibiscus scent wrapped around him and he was very aware of just how alone they were—and of the way her gaze dipped to his mouth, then to his bare chest, and back up to his mouth. Yeah, she'd been watching him the same as he'd been watching her.

He barely held back a groan at the hungry way she was staring because for just a moment her expression was so unguarded, so *hungry*, that he lost all sense.

Without thinking, he leaned forward, closing the distance between them, and just like that she did the same. As he crushed his mouth to hers, he slid his hand through her hair, tugging her ponytail free. He wanted her hair down, wanted her completely open to him as they lost themselves in each other.

She made a little moaning sound as he cupped the back of her head, one that went straight to his dick. And when he nipped at her bottom lip—

The sound of a door opening then shutting tore them apart. *Shit.* His heart rate was already jacked up, but this never should have happened. He should have been paying better attention to their surroundings, should have known they had company.

"Berlin?" It was Adalyn, the one who seemed to be in charge. He still wasn't sure of the hierarchy, but it was clear that everyone followed her orders.

"This was a mistake," Berlin whispered. "I'm sorry, it won't happen again." With incredible speed, she jumped to her feet, grabbed her laptop and practically ran from the room as if he was poison.

Well, then. Feeling as if she'd kicked him in the gut, he rolled to his feet and headed for the stairs. He could take the damn hint. In the room they'd shared, he grabbed his stuff, then dumped it in the room next to hers before jumping in the shower.

He was pretty sure he'd been called a mistake by more than one woman in the past, but never to his face. And he wouldn't have cared. He'd only had one-night stands before. But with Berlin, he'd stupidly allowed himself to think... It didn't matter. Nothing was going to happen between them.

Clearly.

Didn't matter how much he wanted it, that kiss was a mistake. Beyond annoyed with himself, he turned the water to cold as he scrubbed off the sweat of the day. Maybe she was right. Maybe kissing her had been stupid. Because now he wanted to do it again.

But under much different, naked circumstances.

As disappointment slid through him, he told himself that this was for the best. He needed to focus on finding his brother, and getting tangled up with someone was monumentally stupid.

Even if that someone lived in his brain, filled up all his fantasies, made him feel like he might have a different future than he'd ever envisioned. But what did he think was going to happen? If they'd let things go any further, it would have made things complicated. And right now he needed her focused on finding his brother too.

She was right, it had been a mistake. One he wouldn't make again.

Probably.

CHAPTER 17

I came, I saw, I made it awkward.

"Morning," Berlin managed to get out as Chance stepped into the kitchen. She tried to keep her voice normal, and none of the others had looked at her weird so maybe she'd pulled it off? *Fingers crossed.*

"Morning." Chance's voice was deep and delicious and not something she needed to be thinking about, but that one word slid right through to her core. Especially now that she knew what he tasted like, had felt the energy and hunger rolling through him as he'd kissed her back. Not that acting they'd done in front of the Uptown Street Kings, but a real, way-too-short kiss where she'd been ready to strip naked and ride him right in the middle of the living room.

Gah.

After talking to Adalyn last night about what she'd found out, Adalyn had gathered the others and now they had a plan. Everything was so last minute, something Berlin normally hated.

Okay, still did.

But they couldn't wait for another opportunity if the Backwater Bayou Boys were going to make a drug run. According to Hazel, they would be making a run tomorrow so Berlin and the others had to get in place now. She'd felt weird about going to Chance last night to tell him everything—especially after she'd realized he'd moved all his stuff from their shared room.

Of course he had, but still, it had stung. So she'd simply texted him, like a coward, telling him the plan even though only a wall had separated them. That wall might as well be in between them now.

"Coffee smells good," he continued, his voice still annoyingly normal.

Okay, then so...that was good at least. But he still hadn't made eye contact with her.

Inwardly frowning, she tried to keep her expression neutral as she looked at Adalyn. "Are we ready?"

"Yep. Rowan secured a place for us and both SUVs are packed up. I've got the drones like you requested as well as everything we'll need." Sighing slightly, she looked at Chance. "There's no chance we can talk you out of coming with us?"

Berlin cleared her throat. This had been a disagreement she'd had with Adalyn last night and she'd thought they'd settled things. No way were they leaving Chance behind.

"Nope." Chance didn't look up as he screwed on the top to an insulated to-go travel mug.

"For the record, I don't like this," Adalyn continued as Chance met her gaze. "But I also recognize that this isn't a normal job—"

"I appreciate what you guys are doing, but I'm not your client. And I'm guessing I'm better trained than most of your actual clients."

Adalyn's jaw tightened once. "Fair enough. But I want to make it clear that we're not using lethal force."

"Wasn't planning on it."

Berlin held in another sigh that desperately wanted to escape. She'd had this same discussion with Adalyn last night, and while she understood Adalyn's wariness—this was definitely out of the realm of their normal operating procedures—she wished Adalyn trusted her more. Things might be weird between her and Chance but she knew he'd be an asset for this.

"Okay, then we're good," Adalyn said. "Also...if I give an order, I expect you to follow it. We're used to working together as a team and my priority is keeping my people safe and finding your brother. But we don't act like asshole cowboys. Got it?"

Chance nodded at her. "Understood. I won't put anyone in danger." His gaze flicked to Berlin's and for a long, pregnant moment she was caught in those dark eyes.

Until he broke contact, and she swore she could feel the loss of that connection like a physical break. She wanted to talk to him, but had no idea how.

Or what to say.

The kiss last night had been incredible, even if it had been foolish.. But...he brought out a different side of her. One she wanted to explore, even if the timing was quite possibly the worst ever.

"You can ride with me," Rowan said to Chance, clearly not asking.

Chance paused, but nodded, falling into step with the other big man as they headed out the side door.

Adalyn simply said, "You good?"

"Yep." Berlin patted the case she'd slung over her shoulder, which had all her gear and anything she might need for the job.

Anticipation buzzed through her, like with any job, but this one was different for a multitude of reasons. She didn't want to let Chance down, couldn't bear for him to lose his brother.

***

After hours of driving northwest, Berlin glanced around the dusty, swampy surroundings of the one-lane road. "Are you sure you couldn't have just flown us in here?"

Adalyn laughed lightly from the driver's seat. "We have way too much gear, and even if we didn't, there's no good place to land around here."

And they'd have potentially given away their arrival to anyone watching the skies. Which might be happening. "Why did Rowan want Chance to ride with him?" she asked, even though they had to be getting close to their destination. She should have asked earlier, but she hadn't wanted to bring up Chance and... Whatever, apparently this was the day she was a coward.

"Just to get to know him, get a feel for how he'll work with the crew."

"Oh."

"Did you think they were going to haze him or something?"

"Maybe. No. Rowan wouldn't do that."

"Tiago would."

"Yeah...Bradford might too. He's a wild card." And still he was one of her favorites. Maybe that was why. She never knew what to expect from him.

Adalyn snickered. "I know. He's too quiet sometimes. Makes me wonder what he's plotting."

"I'm surprised Ezra didn't want to come today."

"Oh he did, but I made him finish out his honeymoon. He didn't fight me too hard." She cleared her throat pointedly. "Because some people know how to take vacations."

"Oh my god, after we find Chance's brother I'll take a break. For real."

"Hmm. So, who's been texting you this whole drive?"

"Ah...my sisters. One's dealing with a work crisis, the other a romantic one, and Cheyenne is back to believing her boyfriend is cheating on her. Which he definitely is. I hacked his phone records," she added.

Adalyn raised an eyebrow.

"Fine. And his social media. I want to give the info to Cheyenne but I'm second-guessing myself. Is it *really* my business?"

"She's your sister. And if someone was cheating on you, I'd tell you, for the record."

"Yeah but you wouldn't, like, hack his shit," she muttered. "Sometimes I think I really do need better boundaries."

"What? Who the hell is putting this in your head?" Adalyn demanded as they bounced over a pothole. Or maybe it was just a hole considering this was a dirt road through a bunch of woods.

"No one. I think maybe I'm having an identity crisis or something." She groaned at herself and looked out the window at the passing trees. Everything was a blur of green and brown. "Bradford said I needed to put myself first, to figure out who I am. And I honestly don't know if I even know. I'm so used to taking care of my sisters that it feels weird to...not. To pull back. But then I feel guilty for not helping when they ask. Mari has this way of just listening when I talk and it's amazing. It's like she has all her shit figured out and understands social cues and boundaries in a way I'm worried I never will. And now that I've dumped all this on you..." She covered her face, annoyed with herself for the verbal diarrhea. "I'm realizing that now is probably not the time for all this. See? I suck with boundaries."

"First of all, you don't suck at anything. Second, don't compare yourself to Mari, who is awesome, for the record. But you guys had very different upbringings, and if you think she has her shit together... Well you're probably not wrong. But this isn't about her or anyone else. If your sisters ask for advice, give it. But if they're just venting, then listen and commiserate.

That's it."

"You make it sound so easy."

"Of course it's not. It's going to be so hard at first and maybe always. Especially when you can see the writing on the wall in the case of a bad relationship. So if Cheyenne texts you or calls you and says 'oh my god, I think my boyfriend is cheating on me,' what do you say?"

"I feel like threatening to burn his place down to the studs is wrong," she said dryly.

Adalyn snort-laughed. "Well, probably wrong. No, it's definitely wrong. Let's try again. She's not asking for advice. So..."

"So...I say, 'I'm sorry you're worried about him and I'm here for you'?"

"Is that a question?"

"Maybe? No...that's what I say."

"Sounds good to me."

Berlin shook her head slightly. "That's too easy."

"Nope. It's not. Especially when you know the jerk is cheating on her. And sisters are different than other people. There are different rules so some of this won't always apply. And I think you can give her proof that he's cheating on her under certain circumstances. But if she has a pattern of staying with him after she knows he's cheated on her—"

"She does."

"Okay then, she's just venting. What did you say when she texted you?"

"Nothing." Because Berlin was floundering, and questioning everything lately. *Ugh.* She pulled out her phone and reread Cheyenne's text.

I think Toby is cheating on me. He keeps putting his phone down when I walk into a room, and he's ignoring incoming texts when I'm around.

She typed out a response, then reread it a couple of times. *I'm sorry you're struggling right now and I'm here for you.* She wanted to tell Cheyenne so badly that her stupid boyfriend was cheating on her but this was not her first rodeo and she couldn't keep doing the same thing over and over, expecting a different result. She hit send, shoved out a sigh as she leaned back in her seat.

Then Adalyn hit another dip in the road, cursed under her breath. "At least we're almost there."

When Berlin's phone buzzed again, she glanced at the incoming text. It was Cheyenne again. *What do you think I should do?*

"Well now she's asking for advice," she muttered more to herself than Adalyn. Again, she was tempted to give her sister proof of her boyfriend's cheating ways, but her gut told her that was the wrong move. With her other sisters it would be the right move, but with Cheyenne, it would blow up in her face. She texted back again: *Trust your instinct. You have a really smart inner voice who only wants good things for you.*

A moment later Cheyenne texted back a couple heart emojis.

Berlin groaned and tossed her phone down. "It's really hard not telling her the truth."

"She already knows the truth," Adalyn said as they pulled into a clearing with a cabin, a firepit and...

"Oh my god, is that an outhouse?" Berlin stared out the window at the sight before them. "What. The. Hell."

Adalyn just laughed, as if it was hilarious.

"You told me Rowan found us a decent place to stay."

"No, I said he found a hideout not far from an airboat rental place."

Berlin bit back a response as she eyed their surroundings. The cabin looked okay on the outside, but an outhouse? *Gross.* But she'd reserve judgment until later.

Until she discovered if they actually had working plumbing or not.

CHAPTER 18

What doesn't kill you makes you stronger—except gators. Gators will definitely kill you.

Chance tried not to watch Berlin as they unloaded everything from the two SUVs. He'd wanted to talk her this morning, though he'd had no idea what to say. But there'd never been an opportunity. Maybe she was glad for it, considering she thought their kiss was a mistake. He couldn't get her words out of his head even though he wanted nothing more than to pretend she'd never said them.

"Here." Tiago tossed Chance a heavy bag, grinning as he caught it midair.

He grunted under the impact and weight, but hefted it up on one shoulder then snagged another bag for good measure.

Which made Tiago smile even wider as he picked up a small bag.

Berlin raced into the cabin ahead of them, then ran out a second later making a whooping sound. "We have working plumbing!"

"Just don't let Bradford anywhere near it after that chili he ate last night," Tiago grumbled.

"I'll make sure to go before your shower tonight." Bradford took one of the bags from Chance. "And don't let Tiago trick you into carrying everything. He's really good at that."

"Work smarter, not harder," the other man said with a grin as he hurried past them.

Inside, the cabin was about what he'd expected. It looked like an old hunting or fishing cabin. Maybe both. There were two couches, a seventies-era coffee table reminiscent of what his grandmother had owned, and a chunky television with a VCR player next to it. Considering that there wasn't even a DVD player, he assumed streaming was out. The TV was so old he doubted it even had the capability. Not that it mattered—they had too much shit to do today. But it said a lot for how off the grid this place was.

When Tiago set one of the bags on the longer couch, dust puffed out in a thick cloud.

"Ugh, this place blows." Berlin was back inside, coughing a little as she glanced around.

"At least we've got electricity," Chance murmured, because he'd stayed in true hovels before. The worst place he'd ever had to hunker down was somewhere in Venezuela—he still wasn't sure exactly where—for a week while he and his unit waited on orders. They weren't supposed to even be there, so they'd had to go under the radar of literally everyone, which meant they'd had to camp out in the triple canopy jungle with animals that looked like they belonged in sci-fi movies.

"True." She smiled up at him and for a moment it was like last night hadn't happened. Then she clearly remembered, her bright gaze skittering away before she headed for what had to be the bedroom.

Sighing to himself, he dumped his bag next to Tiago's, then headed back outside to help bring in the rest.

Once they were done, Rowan nodded at him. "You come with me."

Surprised, he simply followed the other man into the cool, fresh air and jumped in the front seat when Rowan motioned for him to get in the SUV. "You want me to go with you?" The plan was to rent an airboat, then do recon on the surrounding river system. Which was, unfortunately, complex.

Rowan shrugged. "Why not?"

"Okay, then." He was game, wanted to get out there and be doing something, but was still surprised Rowan wanted him along. He'd expected to be sidelined.

"So how long have you known Berlin?" Rowan asked as he headed back up the dirt path they'd come.

And there was the question he'd been waiting on. Or one of them. He'd expected something on the ride here, but they'd mostly just talked shit to each other and asked him a few questions about the army. But nothing too personal and they hadn't pushed much. He wouldn't have told them anything regardless, which they'd probably known. But the ride had been almost too casual, and he'd been waiting for the anvil to drop.

"Couple years." Something the man already knew. Or Chance assumed he did. He wasn't sure how much Berlin had told him and the others.

Rowan just made a humming sound as he pulled out onto a paved, two-lane road. Everything here was flat, with brush and trees surrounding them. The scent of fresh water was heavy in the air, which made sense since they were surrounded by rivers and lakes. He knew there was something close to five thousand navigable miles of rivers, creeks, canals and other bodies of water in Louisiana. At least they wouldn't have to navigate all of that, but it was still a lot of unexplored terrain to deal with while they tried to find the exact path that the Backwater Bayou Boys used to run their drugs.

"She's like family to us," Rowan continued, as if there hadn't been a giant lull in their conversation.

But Chance had known more was coming. "I'm aware." Even if she hadn't told him about the people she worked with being like family, he'd have been able to tell simply from the protective way everyone was with each other. They all cared about each other in a kind of way that you couldn't fake.

"Figured you did. But I wanted to spell it out."

"Is this the part where you threaten to kill me if I hurt her?"

"If I thought you were here to hurt her, you'd be dead already."

"I respect that. And for the record, I didn't even want her involved in any of this. She was very forceful." The woman was a total bulldozer taking over and...fine, he didn't hate it. He did hate the thought of her in any sort of danger, but with her crew here, at least she wouldn't be near any action. As long as she stayed behind, giving them valuable backup, he could deal with her being involved.

Rowan snorted softly as he pulled off onto another dirt path. "Yeah, she has a habit of doing what she wants, when she wants." To Chance's surprise, he put the SUV in park in the middle of the path, then opened the door.

"What are you doing?" Because they were absolutely nowhere right now. He looked out the windows at the surrounding cypress trees in the shallow water on either side of them. Spanish moss draped the branches, giving shade to any gators lurking beyond the shores.

"Airboat rental place is at the end of this road. I don't want our vehicle on any cameras," he tossed over his shoulder as he headed to the back hatch. "You're gonna drive back down the road, make a left, then another left on that turnoff about a mile back. You remember it?"

"Yeah." Chance was already unbuckling and getting out as Rowan grabbed a ball cap and thicker than normal sunglasses.

"Good. Drive to the end of that turnoff. There's a little riverbank where you can park. I'll pick you up, then we're heading out for that recon."

"All right." Chance still wasn't sure why Rowan had asked him instead of one of his teammates, but he was glad to be doing something active.

Maybe that was the reason... Or more likely he'd just wanted to keep an eye on Chance. Whatever it was, he had to believe they were closer to finding Enzo.

***

Sure enough, ten minutes later, Rowan pulled up in a rush of manmade wind, the airboat gliding up onto the sandy shore. He had a couple fishing poles he must have rented, plus a bucket of bait—all part of their cover in case they ran into any trouble.

Chance jumped onto the front, found his footing as Rowan reversed and took off. He'd been on airboats before and the sensation was always like flying. He tucked his ball cap in his back pocket so it wouldn't fly off but kept his sunglasses on.

Wordlessly Rowan handed him the GPS, so Chance took over as Rowan steered away from the shore. On the drive over, despite the trash talk and other nonsense, they'd gone over the plan to scour for any signs of drug running.

As they flew down the river, Berlin called, and just like that his heart skipped a beat.

"Hey, can you hear me?" Chance shouted over the noise.

"Yeah, but it's noisy. Put your earbuds in. They should cancel some of the noise."

He slid them both in. "How about now?"

"Much better. I'm monitoring your trackers as they move. See anything good yet?"

"No, but we just left. How are you settling in?" It was a lot easier to talk to her over the phone. It had barely been a few hours since they'd truly talked and he'd been sleeping for most of them, but he still missed her voice.

"Ugh. Fine. But this place is gross."

"So you're not into camping, I take it?"

"Double gross. Why would I make the conscious choice to sleep on the ground in a bag? Just why?"

He laughed at her description, even though he loved disconnecting out in the wild. "It's not all bad. So what do you see on your end?" She was keeping track of them and would be giving them intel on the drive.

"Hold on…" She was quiet for a long few moments, but he was just glad they were talking normally again.

"What's Berlin say?" Rowan asked as he neared a split in the river. He slowed down, and the water rippled out in both directions.

The water rocked them gently as Chance held up a finger. "She's working."

"Okay, if you head to the right," she finally said, "You'll end up in a lake that looks as if it gets fished a lot. I'm going back through past satellite images, various social media feeds and other stuff, and it seems as if not only is it a good fishing spot, but people boat and party that way as well. I can't imagine anyone runs drugs through there. So take the left bend. It stretches for about ten miles north."

He motioned for Rowan to head that way and he did without another word. She'd already looked up some of this stuff last night and he imagined she had as well on the drive here, but knew she was still working on piecing together an accurate picture of the places they should check out and the ones that weren't worth their time. Thanks to her mystery contact, they already had a pretty good idea of who the Boys delivered to, but there was too much open water to the east for them to nail down the drop-off location.

That meant they had to figure out at least part of the path the gang took beforehand in the twine of rivers and bayou. So they were looking for a needle in a stack of needles.

About twenty minutes later, a text popped up with an image of where he and Rowan were and a red line showing exactly which direction they should take. "If I was going to run drugs," Berlin said, "and was coming in from the west, this is the path I'd take. It's pretty rough and there are some areas that I can't quite see from satellite images to know enough if they're open to boaters. So you'll have to check it in person. This could be a bust," she added. "Just want to make that clear. There's a lot of terrain to travel and I'm trying to think like a criminal."

He held it out to Rowan so he could see the GPS. "We have enough gas to make it?"

"Yeah, we're good."

"Thanks Berlin, this is great."

"Like I said—"

"Even if it doesn't work out, this is incredible and we're closer than we were. Just...thank you." He wanted to tell her exactly how incredible she was, but not with an audience and not shouting it over the rush of the wind and engine.

"If anything looks different on your end from these images let me know and I'll work on mapping out another path."

"Will do."

Once they disconnected, it was quiet save for the boat as they rushed over the water. The wind and sun beat against his face, but he'd worn a long-sleeved shirt to stave off most of the heat.

An hour later, Rowan slowed as they reached a narrowing in one of the river branches they'd taken. At this point they'd traveled through almost two dozen river branches that ended up being dead ends. There was simply too much terrain for them to manage.

But as Rowan slowed along another branch of water, he frowned as he took in their surroundings, shallow waters below them and mangrove and cypress trees on either side of them.

The engine idled as they drifted closer to a blockage in the path. A cluster of mangrove trees looked as if they'd been ripped up, maybe from a storm. But they were more or less neatly stacked on each other, blocking an upcoming path that their boat could just get through if it was clear.

Rowan crouched down to look in the bucket of bait, kept his voice pitched so low that Chance barely heard it over the engine. "Play along with what I say."

And that was when Chance saw the cameras in the trees. Not the cheap kind hunters left to check later for signs of wildlife, but the kind that were actively monitored.

"That asshole lied to us," Rowan snarled as he glanced at the trees blocking their way. "This isn't a secret fishing hole."

Chance cursed in agreement as he slid his ball cap on. "Man, he saw us coming."

The two of them grumbled a bit more before Rowan reversed out of the shallow waters and headed back down the waterway.

As they cruised, Chance clocked two more high-end cameras, but didn't look directly at them. Only once they were about three miles out did they slow again, then park on one of the sandy banks.

There was a camera about fifty yards to the north of them so Chance figured he knew what Rowan was doing. Sure enough, he started baiting the fishing poles for the two of them before they waded into a little channel carved out by another river branch or maybe past flooding. Now it was a pool of largemouth bass ripe for picking.

For the next hour they talked sports, about the fictional women in their lives, drank beers, and fished. Chance kept his ball cap and sunglasses on just as Rowan did, and they mostly angled their faces away from the direction of the cameras.

But they had to maintain the cover of two guys fishing for the rest of the afternoon. Eventually Rowan said, "Let's see if we can find another spot."

Then they headed out, but not before marking the location. Even then, they took their time heading back to where Rowan had originally picked up Chance.

"So?" Chance said once Rowan had pulled up onto the sand, the engine of the airboat quiet.

"That was some serious, waterproof hardware. Not the kind hobby fishermen or hunters use."

"Yeah, someone's watching that area. So we can't hit any potential runners there."

"Nope. But we can keep an eye on it aerially and set up about five miles south."

Chance nodded. "The cameras start to thin about that mark. If anything, we could knock one out if necessary, but I think we've got a good enough stretch where we can set up an ambush." He looked down at the map of where they'd been, zoomed in, pointed. "Right here."

"That's exactly what I was thinking. And if they're making a run tomorrow, I say we head back out here tonight and just wait."

Chance nodded again, because it was better to set up and be ready than to head out tomorrow and be too late.

CHAPTER 19

"See, camping isn't so bad," Chance murmured as he sat in one of the Adirondack chairs next to Berlin.

Laptop on her legs, she took her wireless headset off and glanced at him. "Sitting by a campfire is fun. Making s'mores is fun. Sleeping in a dusty bag...not so much." You know, unless she was curled up with *him*—but she kept that thought to herself. Because she would absolutely make an exception for camping if they got to be naked together.

He and Rowan had gotten back not long ago, and everyone was currently sitting around the firepit while Tiago made them all s'mores. Soon most of them would head out to get in place but not until closer to midnight.

"It's fun in the winter. It can be amazing just sleeping out under the stars next to a campfire." He said it with a kind of wistfulness that told her he was remembering doing just that.

"Honestly, this is the kind of stuff you should keep to yourself," she murmured.

He snickered, then shook his head at Tiago when he offered him another s'more. "I'm good, but thanks. And," he said, looking back at Berlin, "I bet I can change your mind. After...all this." His expression dimmed slightly as he glanced at the fire.

"We're going to find your brother." She hated making promises, and wasn't exactly making one, but...she wanted to help him, no matter what the ending of this was. She was tempted to reach out, comfort him, but resisted the urge. Now definitely wasn't the time. Though she wanted to say more, she heard voices through her headset so she slid it back on her head. And realized this was what they'd been waiting for. "Hey, everyone listen up." She waved her hand once then turned the Bluetooth off so they could all hear the incoming call to Armand Loutrel, owner of Armand's Airboats which Rowan had rented from today. Hacking his line had been ridiculously easy.

"Tell me about the men who rented the airboat from you today." The man who'd called Armand had a slight Texas twang—which lined up with any one of the Acton brothers, who all allegedly hailed from Texas.

"I rented a lot of boats today." Now that was pure Louisiana Cajun accent.

Berlin looked over at Rowan, who was crouched in front of the firepit. "Is this the same guy from the rental place? His voice?"

"Sounds like it. Can barely understand him," he muttered, shaking his head.

Berlin had been monitoring Armand's phone on the off chance he worked with any of the traffickers. It was an educated guess and made sense that these runners would work with locals. It was the same the world over. Because eyes on the ground were a lot more useful than cameras that could break or be hacked.

"I'm talking specifically about two men, both large, white-looking. They were out fishing and drinking beer, got real close to one of our routes. That would've been around two."

"I rented seven boats today and none to two men. But one fella mentioned pickin' up a friend. Coulda been them."

"Did you tell him about any fishing spots?"

"Course I did. He wasn't too bright though."

Tiago and Bradford snickered, but Rowan simply rolled his eyes.

"Anything about him seem off?"

"Nah. But I won't be surprised if he gets himself killed out there. He rented a boat for three days, says he plans to fish the whole time and drink his weight in beer."

"Why'd you rent to him, then?"

Now the man guffawed. "If I didn't rent to dumbasses, I'd have no customers. He paid with a card. You want the information, or you want to keep hassling me with questions?"

The other man's voice was tight as he responded. "Yes, send me his credit card and ID. And if you think of anything else, let me know. Someone will be by in a week to pay you."

"Alrighty."

The other man disconnected in response. The owner muttered to himself for a moment before the call ended.

"At least we know the fake ID will hold up," Berlin said. They had a multitude of cover IDs complete with background information. And none of the IDs ever had their real faces on them. They'd all been slightly edited so that if anyone ran the ID picture, what they'd find was a carefully curated social media history.

Rowan's ID from today was that of an Oliver Johnson from Baton Rouge who liked posting fishing memes, political rants and had a spotty job history. It would hold up under scrutiny and shouldn't invite any more questions.

"They work fast," she continued as a search popped up for the fake ID.

Everyone was quiet for a moment, but eventually they started murmuring among themselves as she watched the screen.

"I feel like I already know the answer, but can you do anything with the phone number that called Armand Loutrel?" Chance asked.

She shook her head. "I already ran it. It's a burner. Don't get me wrong, I'll see if I can dig deeper, but these guys are careful. It's going to be a dead end."

Sighing, he stood. "Yeah, I figured."

She wished she could comfort him or...something. But things were still weird between them and right now the priority was finding Enzo. Besides, she couldn't have a conversation with him about their kiss in front of everyone. As Chance stalked off into the darkness toward the water instead of back to the cabin, she forced herself to focus on her laptop.

She traced the searches for Oliver Johnson, followed them all back to what turned out to be a ranch house in Houston. She made a note of the location for now, because there wasn't much they could do with it at the moment. Once it was clear she wasn't getting any more useful information, she slid her laptop onto the seat then headed in the direction Chance had gone—ignoring the looks she got from Adalyn and Rowan.

"Hey, want company?" she sat down next to Chance on a patch of sandy shore.

"Sure." He had his knees pulled up, his elbows propped up on them as he stared out into the darkness.

The river and lake beyond looked almost black to her, even under the moonlight and stars. "They looked into Rowan's fake ID. That's a good thing."

"Yeah, I know. I'm just thinking about my brother, that's all. I just can't see him getting tangled up with drug runners."

"People are complicated."

He snorted softly. "That's a diplomatic response."

She stretched her legs out and sighed. "Sorry, I'm not sure what to say."

"You don't need to say anything. You're already doing a hell of a lot," he murmured. "Without you...honestly, I don't know where I'd be. I also don't know that I even deserve your help."

"Your brother is missing. This isn't about deserving help. We all need it sometimes."

"Yeah well...my relationship with Enzo isn't the best. The last time we talked we said a lot of shitty things to each other. He blamed me for a lot."

When it was clear that he was done, Berlin nudged him slightly. "Want to air it out? Talk about it?"

"No...but he wasn't wrong about some of it. I left home as soon as I was able. My sister...died way too young. My grandma tried her best. We all did. I tried to earn enough money to pay for her treatment but..." He ran a hand over his face, sighed. "After she died, I just had to get out of there," he muttered. "I loved my brother, and maybe I should have stayed. But I felt like I was suffocating in that shithole of a town. And now I realize that saying this to you of all people just shows how selfish I was." He turned away from her to stare back out at the water.

The wind kicked up, blowing her hair back and sending a shiver down her spine. "Our situations were different, and there's no right answer for stuff like that. You were eighteen when you left, a kid yourself. You'd lost your sister and had to have been grieving. And at the end of the day, you can't take responsibility for your brother's actions."

"Maybe, maybe not. My grandmother was there for him and she tried hard, but..." He shook his head.

Scooting closer, she laid her head on his shoulder. She wished she could comfort him more, but wasn't sure he'd want her touch.

He tensed for a moment, but seconds later she could feel that tension leaving his body as he leaned into her. "I don't like the thought of leaving you behind while we head out tonight."

"I know, but I'll be fine."

"You're just saying that so you don't have to sleep on a boat." His tone was dry.

She laughed lightly. "That boat is a better option than the cabin."

"So says you. One day I'm going to get you out camping and sleeping under the stars."

She sat there a moment, debating her next words and then just decided to throw them out there. "You still want to be friends after all this?" she asked, because he'd seemed to have one foot out the door since she'd rolled into his life like a bulldozer. Because apparently that was what she did. *Boundaries, schmoundaries.*

"Of course I still want to be friends," he growled far too sexily. As he did, he shifted slightly, forcing her to look up at him. "Why would you even ask that?"

"I don't know... I sort of busted into your real life and made you take my help. I know I can be a lot."

"You're not a lot, you're absolutely perfect, Berlin." Again with that sexy growl that curled through her, making her want far too much.

Her eyebrows shot up at that but he didn't take the words back. And she loved when he said her name. "Seriously?"

"Jesus, Berlin, yeah. You're perfect and it's intimidating being your friend."

She slow blinked at that. No one had ever called her perfect before, much less twice in a row. She'd been called "a lot" or "extra" by her sisters more times than she could count. Maybe it was a sister thing but sometimes she wondered.

"And for the record, if I hadn't wanted your help, I could have just snuck out that first night and left. You're not holding me hostage. I'm here willingly, and grateful for your help."

"Well that's another thing, I don't want you to be grateful and—"

He gave a low curse and dipped his head, crushing his mouth over hers in a swift, searing claiming. Because this was more than a kiss. He teased his tongue against hers as he slid his hand against her jaw, behind her head, cupped her tight.

God, she loved how he held on to her, as if he was afraid she'd bolt. Which to be fair, she was considering. Because this felt way too complicated. She was finding it hard to care though as heat slid low in her belly, expanding out to all of her as he kissed her slow, and long and...oh, he tugged her onto his lap so that she was straddling him.

And she loved the feel of being on top of him as they explored each other's mouths. She traced the raised scar along his left jawline and—

"Oh, shit." The sound of Bradford's voice broke them apart and by the time she managed to pull back and glance behind Chance, Bradford was already booking it in the other direction.

She winced slightly, but whatever. She didn't think Bradford would tell everyone what he'd just seen. And she was an adult; she could do whatever the hell she wanted.

"It's probably getting close to time to get out of here." Chance stood then, held out a hand for her. Instead of letting her go when she was on her feet, he pulled her flush against his body, slid his arms around her and held tight. "And for the record, I don't regret this and don't think it's a mistake."

CHAPTER 20

*Good or bad, what you put out there comes
back to you.*

Chance watched the screen of Tiago's drone swooping high above the cypress trees. They'd set up in place a couple of hours ago, with the airboat tucked away near a makeshift beach hidden by mangrove trees and underbrush. They'd tied a rope to one of the trees after setting up a special surprise for any potential drug runners.

At this point he wasn't sure any of this would matter, but he was still hopeful that it would help find Enzo. He'd already lost his sister. He couldn't lose his brother too.

He heard the buzz of the engine even before the dark screen lit up with the incoming boats.

A couple hours after midnight, it was quiet out in the spiderweb of surrounding rivers and lakes. It was too late and they were too far out for this to be random boaters. No one with any sense would be out here unless they were up to something.

Chance watched as Tiago maneuvered the drone, impressed with his skills. His friend Hot Shot had a remote drone certification and had been putting his skills to use behind enemy lines for the last five years. Chance wondered if Tiago had done the same at one time.

"You're really good with that."

"Thanks," Tiago said as he flew a little lower. "Takes a lot of practice. And this one is really sensitive, but I love her anyway."

Chance snorted softly, then stilled as another boat came into view. They hadn't been planning on a big entourage. Normally drug runners kept their runs light, so if they had to escape it was a lot easier to lose pursuers. He knew that Miami and South American drug runners tended to use Donzis but it appeared that these guys were using airboats. Which made sense for the shallow waterways here.

Chance pulled up the simple handheld radio Rowan had given him earlier before he and Adalyn had been dropped off up river about half a mile. "Two airboats en route, about two miles from your spot."

Rowan responded. "How many tangos?"

"Seven...eight." A man stepped out from behind another one, revealing a separate heat signature. With the night vision, they were working with heat signatures. "Looks like harpoons stacked up on the first boat."

"Yeah," Tiago murmured, getting a little lower as he kept pace with the boat. "Could be gator hunters, given all the harpoons." Tiago couldn't get too low with the drone because they might be seen, but also because of the airflow from the airboat. It would disrupt the drone too much, potentially causing a crash.

"Doubt it," Chance said. "It's too late—or early—to be out. And two of the guys in the back are armed."

"How can you tell?" Tiago frowned at the screen even as he maneuvered the controls with an ease that spoke of a lot of practice.

"Look at the angles of their arms." Their arms mostly looked like blobs, but they could differentiate them enough to separate them from their bodies. Especially the two guys in the back of the boat. "They're holding something long and awkward. My money's on something semiautomatic."

"Yeah, you're probably right. Considering the harpoons, I'm guessing they're posing as gator hunters in case they get caught."

"The others will be armed too." Going on past experience, Chance figured the whole gang would be carrying similar weapons or MAC-10s. They were lighter and easier to aim and had been a favorite of traffickers for decades. Though in his experience they tended to miss more than they hit. "Everyone in place?"

"We're good," Rowan said. "You just watch Tiago's back."

Chance bristled slightly but knew it wasn't personal. They didn't know him enough to be sure of his skills.

"We're going to let the first boat past the checkpoint," Adalyn said as the buzz of the engines grew louder. "Then as soon as the second boat is lined up, it's on."

That was code for "we're blowing shit up."

Chance released the rope on the boat and had his weapon out. And just like the others, he was covered in various shades of dark greens and brown body paint. They'd all geared up on the ride over and were wearing similar shades of clothing, their faces and necks camouflaged.

Adalyn and Rowan were nearest to Chance and Tiago, with Bradford a mile up the river providing backup from the rear. Chance had wanted to take point with him, but Adalyn was in charge and had made it clear that he'd be on the boat with Tiago.

And since they were all out here in the middle of the bayou helping him at two something in the morning against a bunch of drug runners, he was going to listen. Even if it went against all his instincts to be right in the middle of the fray.

Tiago was pulling the drone back in now. "Get ready," he murmured to Chance, who was already at the wheel, ready to turn the boat back on.

In the distance, an explosion blasted through the relative quiet, drowning out the sound of the engines as orange flames licked into the sky.

He flipped on the ignition, kicked the boat into drive and tore out of the hidden bay. As he rounded out into the river branch, a picture of chaos opened up in front of them.

The first boat was tipped on its side with Adalyn and Rowan taking care of the men on it—shouting orders and holding weapons on them. The other boat had turned around, but gunfire erupted from what was now the front of them where Bradford was.

The men returned fire in a staccato that was all too familiar to Chance. Tiago was at the front, holding his own weapon up and firing on the back cage of the retreating airboat as Chance sped up on them from behind.

"Brace," he called out as the airboat started to turn, clearly realizing they were being fired upon from behind.

He didn't pause, but rammed into them at an angle as Tiago held tight. The blow shoved them up into a cluster of mangrove tree roots. As the engine suddenly cut off, Chance motioned to Tiago what he was doing and slid off the side of the boat into the cold waters.

Tiago did the same, moving quietly and quickly through the dark river alongside Chance.

"What the hell is going on?" someone snarled.

"I can't get a hold of Javier." This from someone else.

Gunfire erupted, bullets slamming into the airboat they'd left behind. Chance slid under the water when a flashlight swung in their direction, then surfaced quietly as the light skittered away. He absolutely hated being in dark waters like this, but it was the only way to get to these guys unseen.

Two men were standing on the port side of the boat, flashlights and weapons up as they scanned beyond the mangrove trees, trying to figure out where the gunfire had come from and where Chance and Tiago were.

Chance swam up to the opposite side of the boat with Tiago and plastered himself below the hull, waiting for the men to move back to this side.

He'd seen one fallen body and had heard someone else splash into the water earlier but there was nothing to do about them now. He just hoped Bradford had a handle on the missing guy and took him out.

He pulled his kukri out, the black, epoxy-coated blade not glinting under any of the ambient light as they waited for the tangos to move back to searching the waters for them.

Their bootsteps thudded on the metal deck, their flashlights swinging back over the water in the direction Chance and Tiago had swum in from. Chance leaned back slightly, looked up and made his move.

He stabbed through the guy's left boot with his switchblade and reached around with his kukri, slicing his Achilles in a long-practiced move. The man screamed in agony, his weapon clattering to the deck as he stumbled forward.

Chance used his momentum and yanked the guy into the water, while next to him Tiago had shoved the other guy backward and was climbing onto the boat. A blade glinted under the moonlight, the only warning Chance got before the guy attempted to stab him.

But he was too slow, likely in too much pain, and Chance's adrenaline had spiked. He grabbed his wrist, twisted until he felt the snap and had the guy in a headlock before the man knew what was happening.

His body had likely gone into shock because of the amount of pain and stress and it didn't take long for Chance to knock him unconscious. By the time he hauled the guy's dead weight to shore, Bradford was pushing another guy down the gravelly shoreline to them. This one was at least walking of his own accord, but his arms were bound behind his back and he looked ready to kill.

Chance laid his guy down, then bound his wrists and feet as Bradford ordered the other man to lie down next to his friend.

Tiago jumped off the boat, his boots splashing as he made his way to them. "One's restrained and the other's shot, but he'll be all right if he gets medical attention."

Chance and Bradford both nodded but were otherwise silent as Chance motioned that he was going to swim back to their boat and radio the others. He didn't say anything aloud, simply used hand gestures they understood.

Once he was on the boat, he radioed Adalyn. "SITREP?"

"All tangoes down, boat unusable, and a whole lot of drugs in the hull. They've got a fake bottom."

"I'll check this one and head to you guys. Same situation here, all tangos are incapacitated, with one of them shot. Four says he should make it if he gets medical." They were using numbers as their call signs so as to not give anything away about themselves.

After she said "copy", he turned the boat back on and headed over to the other one, tied off and jumped on it. He was surprised it was still working after the gunfire it had taken but they must not have done any damage to the engine. Once he was on the other airboat, he found a small drill they'd tucked into one of the coolers and put it to good use. And sure enough, there were a whole lot of hidden drugs and cash in this hull as well.

Given the amount of drugs and the use of two boats, this felt like more than a normal run, so these guys were going to be screwed once they didn't check in.

"Load them up," he called out and Tiago and Bradford dumped the men onto their own boat.

Tiago got behind the wheel of their airboat and Chance jumped back onto their rental. To his surprise, the lone man who was still conscious wasn't cursing or shouting threats at them. No, he was being very quiet, which was interesting.

Chance just wasn't sure if that was a good or bad thing yet.

CHAPTER 21

*It's hard to feel sorry for people when they
get what they deserve.*

Adalyn watched as her husband stalked toward the two men who were awake and propped up against a tree root, water lapping around them.

The water was dark too and she knew they were likely wondering if a gator or something else would swoop up and get them. Which was a possibility, but not a huge one considering all the noise and destruction they'd just made.

They looked up at Rowan defiantly, but she could see the fear in their eyes. And the dark-haired one on the left broke eye contact first, glancing around at the grim surroundings.

Because they were in the middle of nowhere, no one to hear their screams. Something their hindbrains were very aware of. The remaining men had all been dumped on the boat not tipped on its side.

As Adalyn approached, Rowan stepped back, standing at attention. She could see the surprise on their faces, that she was the one in charge. Like the others, she had on camouflage face paint, but she'd tucked her hair under a dark cap to hide the color. There was no hiding she was a woman, but her hair was memorable so it had to be covered.

She crouched down in front of the two of them, then without pause, sprayed the more defiant one in the face with bear spray. Her friend and sometimes coworker, Hailey, had turned her on to its uses. Back when she'd been with the Company, she'd used much more refined methods to get the information she wanted.

But sometimes you had to do what you had to do.

The guy screamed, thrashing around, desperate to wash off his eyes but unable to.

She looked up at Rowan, nodded once and he slapped tape over the guy's mouth as she focused on his friend who was quietly watching her, fear in his dark eyes.

"This is bear spray," she said, holding up the canister. "Nasty stuff. If I don't wash it out soon, he'll go blind. And if you don't tell me what I want, I'll do the same to you. Then I'll leave all of you out here as gator bait. I doubt your bodies will ever be recovered."

"Bitch, you don't know who you're messing with—"

"I do, in fact, know who you are. We know all about your little 'Boy' gang and how you're basically runners for the Acton brothers."

At the mention of the Acton brothers, the guy shifted nervously, water lapping around him in little waves.

"So now that we've established that I know what I'm talking about, you're going to answer my questions."

He made a move as if he was going to spit on her, and faster than she could track, Rowan kicked out, slamming his boot into the guy's gut.

"That would be a mistake," Rowan growled as the guy gasped for breath. "I'm allowing you one. And there are more of you so I'll just slit your throat and be done with you if you try anything like that again."

The man nodded even as he continued gasping for breath. Rowan had probably broken a rib or two, knowing his strength.

She looked up at him, eyebrows raised. That hadn't been part of the plan.

"No one spits on you," he said in response to her unspoken words.

And okay, she loved that he cared about that. She looked back at the man. "So, Eugene—"

He jerked slightly when she said his name.

"Oh yes, we know all of your names, where you live, the names of your relatives, wives, side pieces, everyone. So please keep that in mind when you answer my first question. You work for the Acton brothers. How do you think they're going to react to you losing all their drugs?"

He simply swallowed hard.

"And if you think that anyone knows about this, you would be wrong. Because all of your cameras died right before that explosion went off. It'll look like a glitch. But then later, the Acton brothers are going to find evidence that you and your gang double-crossed them. Unless you tell me what I want to know."

"Okay," he said, looking briefly at his friend who was still moaning, his face red, snot and tears streaking the masking tape over his mouth.

"Someone stole a lot of money from our boss. And he wants it back. Enzo Hendrix is the thief we're looking for."

The guy blinked in surprise. "You want to know about that bastard?" he snarled. "He stole from the Acton brothers too! A whole truck! Everyone's talking about it!"

Okay *now* they were getting somewhere. "What did they do to him?"

"They can't find him. Guy's like a ghost."

"What about his family? We've tried locating them but couldn't find anyone." She had to throw suspicion off his family, namely Chance.

"I don't know." Eugene was already shaking his head as he answered. "We just know they're pissed. But if you can't find his family, then they probably can't either."

"I need contact information for the Acton brothers."

The man blinked. "What?"

"Contact. Information. My people have been unable to procure contact information for the Acton brothers. And we're very good at what we do."

Eugene swallowed hard. Once. Twice. "They don't...they don't really do technology. They're paranoid about being tracked." He let out a bitter laugh as he looked around. "Maybe not so paranoid."

"How do you contact them?"

He looked over at his friend, then past Adalyn to the boat where the rest of his gang was waiting. They were well out of earshot, but he lowered his voice as he said, "TikTok."

She blinked. "What?"

"There are ten different bands unaffiliated with them that they leave random comments on. Only the comments aren't random at all, they're like a code."

That was some serious tradecraft, but Adalyn refused to be impressed by it.

"Whenever I need to contact them, I leave a comment under one of the bands' recent posts. They must have, like, someone checking all the time, because I usually get a response within four hours of any request."

She looked up at Rowan, nodded once toward the other guy.

Her husband hauled him off toward the boat, then she pulled out a blade. Eugene flinched away from her, but she simply said, "I'm going to cut you free and then you're going to write down everything I want to know."

It took twenty minutes, but he wrote down everything he could remember, then showed her on his cell phone so she knew he wasn't lying.

They'd be able to reach out or at least track the Acton brothers now. Or attempt to. But they had a way to contact them, which had been the goal.

When they were finished, she tied him back up.

"I thought you were going to let me go."

"I never said that," she said as she stood. "But I'm also not going to kill you."

"If the Acton brothers find out I talked—"

Rowan hauled him to his feet as Adalyn said, "They will never hear about this from us. We're ghosts as far as you're concerned."

As Rowan dumped him on the airboat with the others, she saw that her crew had left the drugs, but taken all the cash—and disabled the second boat. Yeah, these guys weren't going anywhere. She pulled out a burner, dropped a pin on their location for Camila, then tossed the phone into the hollowed-out hull with the rest of the drugs.

They could make a deal with the Feds if one was offered, or they would go to jail. She didn't care either way. She had what she needed and now they were one step closer to finding Chance's brother.

She wasn't sure if she'd have taken this job on if it hadn't been for Berlin's connection, but as it was, they were going to see this thing through to the end.

CHAPTER 22

*If you always play it safe, eventually you're
going to lose.*

Berlin stepped into the living room to find Chance doing sit-ups. Because of course he was. "Camila is here, just wanted to give you a heads-up."

They'd returned from the job out in the middle of nowhere hours ago after letting Camila know where all the drugs and drug runners were—and she'd contacted the Feds. Thankfully the guy who'd been shot was going to be fine. Not that Berlin particularly cared, but he'd be doing jail time.

Chance rolled up to his feet in a ridiculously sexy move, falling in step with her. He wasn't even out of breath and she had no doubt he'd been on sit-up eight billion or something. Seriously, his biceps deserved a movie of their own, showcasing their raw beauty. Okay, she was officially punch drunk. Apparently she needed more sleep. Or...to get naked with him.

Since they'd returned, they'd both slept, since neither had gotten any the night before. She'd woken a few hours ago and had started a deep dive using the information Eugene Landry had provided. She wasn't sure if Camila showing up in person was a good or bad thing.

"Hey." Berlin opened the side door of the kitchen. "You drive your work car?"

"Yeah, but it's unmarked."

Berlin nodded and handed her a burner phone. "We've been giving you a lot of anonymous tips lately, and even though you already use a burner with us, I figured it wouldn't hurt to start using another one. That way if the Feds get curious, they won't be able to find anything."

Camila gave her a dry look. "I think they're just so happy to be closing so many cases they're going to call it a win, but it's time to switch out my burner anyway," she said as she slid it into her purse. "You good to talk?"

"Yeah." Berlin smothered a yawn trying to escape as she sat at the kitchen table. "You hungry or thirsty?" she asked even as Chance pulled out three bottles of water from the fridge.

"Nah, I'm good and just stopping by since you were on my way to the station. The Feds are very happy with the bust and my boss pulled me in to congratulate me on my resources, so thank you." She sat across from Berlin as Chance sat next to her.

Despite what she'd said, he slid a water over to Camila and gave one to Berlin.

"Are they flipping on anyone up the food chain?"

"Sounds like two of them might in exchange for WITSEC but the majority of them are staying quiet. They're too scared of the Acton brothers—as they should be. Those guys don't play by any civilized rules and they're ghosts."

"Maybe not anymore."

"What have you found?"

"Nothing. *Yet.*" Berlin took a swig of her water, realized just how thirsty she was.

"I wish you'd tell me why you're interested in them." Camila's gaze shot to Chance, but his expression remained carefully neutral. "Nothing from you either?"

He just shrugged.

"You make me crazy, Berlin. But I can't complain." She looked between the two of them, then sighed. "Okay, I know I'm not getting anything else out of you. Oh, but I did get a lead on Johnny Moore."

Berlin had too, but she simply nodded politely. "Yeah?"

"He's... Oh my god, you already know this, don't you?"

Berlin grinned slightly. "Yeah. It seems as if he headed out to California to stay with his sister for a while. At least according to his credit card records." And his sister's social media. Johnny's sister had recently posted about being excited that her big brother was coming to visit and Johnny's credit cards were carving a path out west relatively slowly so it looked like he was taking his bike out there.

"There's a warrant out on him now but that's not my problem."

"Warrant?"

"Brody Williams flipped on him too, even though it incriminated him. He's flipping on everyone at this point."

"No honor among thieves," Chance murmured.

"No, indeed." Camila stood. "Thank you for the water and the help. If you decide to do anything stupid, please let me know so I can talk you out of it."

Berlin just grinned. "Will do."

Once she was gone, Berlin yawned again.

"Have you found anything yet?" Chance asked. "Not that I'm rushing you."

"I know you're not. This is your brother we're looking for. And maybe. I've been following a couple conversations on TikTok I'm pretty sure are code for different drops. One of them is here in New Orleans so I think we should check it out—not stop them. I don't want to get tangled with the Acton brothers just yet. But if we can get eyes on some of these mythical 'brothers' we'll be able to get real names. And that's how we'll be able to track them. They're smart, but if I have their real names, it'll be easier to track their online movements."

"Is that how you found me?"

"You're still asking about that?"

"Of course I'm asking about that. It's making me wonder if any past enemies can track me through VR."

"I didn't find you through your real name. I found your real name through your VR handle. And unless your enemies know that you game, I think you're safe."

"You're going to tell me one day," he grumbled.

"We'll see."

"It sounds like you're good to return to your place if you want," he said into the quiet. "And I've still got mine rented out."

"I think we should call your place a wash, especially since Brody and Johnny both know about it. I don't care if Johnny is headed to California or that Brody's flipped on his people. All the more reason for you to lie low. He's petty and vindictive."

"If he commits any crimes after flipping, he'll lose his deal," Chance said.

She nodded, because that was standard. "Is there anyone back home you're worried about? Relatives or old friends?"

He shook his head. "There's no one back there for me. I'd actually started to pack up my grandmother's house. My house," he amended. "Still feels weird to think of it as my own."

"Your grandmother didn't leave it to both you and your brother?"

"No, probably because she knew he'd squander it away. But I'm going to sell it then give him half the profits if we ever find him."

"We will. PI work just takes time and it sounds like the Acton brothers don't know where he is so I'm calling that a win."

"You guys aren't PIs." His tone was dry.

"Eh, potato, potatoh."

"So you guys just...help people who need it. For free? Is that why your people scooped up all that cash at the scene?" There was a tone in his voice she wasn't sure about.

They'd left the drugs for the Feds to deal with, but taken the money. "Sort of. Some of our clients pay but most don't. And we use any 'free money' like that to take care of overhead or to help people get a fresh start."

"People?"

"Usually women escaping their abusers after the system has failed them. For the record, I think a lot of the system works, but a whole lot of it doesn't. So I don't see the point in playing by other people's rules when they're not following it themselves. Especially when I can help people with my morally gray world view." She pushed up from her chair, exhausted and a little annoyed.

"Are you under the impression that I'm judging you? Because I'm not. I admire you." He stood with her, but instead of giving her space, he stalked toward her until she found herself pressed up against the nearest countertop. "Also, we haven't talked about our kiss—kisses."

She swallowed hard as she looked up at him, wondering at the turn in mood—but not hating it. "What's there to say?" she whispered, all her annoyance being replaced with something else.

"Am I still a mistake?" His words were practically a growl as his gaze fell on her lips.

"I didn't say..." She cleared her throat even as heat curled through her. The way he was watching her... She was about to melt. "I didn't mean that."

"What did you mean?" A soft demand.

Her gaze fell to his mouth now and she could barely remember her name, let alone his question. On instinct, her tongue darted out to moisten her lips, and that was all it took for him. Apparently he didn't care about the answer as he leaned down, crushed his mouth to hers.

He claimed her in that hungry way of his she felt all the way to her core.

Feeling almost manic, she grabbed onto the front of his shirt. They'd already been interrupted twice, and at this point she didn't care if anyone walked in on them. She didn't want to stop whatever this was, wherever it was going. For however long.

But Chance was taking this kiss slow, teasing, gently stroking his tongue against hers, and she was about to combust. Though the reaction she felt from him told her that she wasn't alone in her response.

"Can we take this upstairs?" she managed to murmur against his mouth. Because she didn't want to stop.

Pulling back, he looked down at her in surprise.

"In case anyone shows up and we're interrupted again," she whispered, feeling her cheeks heat up. "Not that I'm, like...pressuring you for more than kisses." She'd just sort of assumed that was where this was headed. She rarely hooked up with guys; couldn't remember the last time she had. But this was different. She knew Chance in a way she didn't know others she'd dated.

She'd opened up to him over the years because it had been easy, behind her headset, to be raw, honest. And now she wondered if she'd made a mistake.

But the way he grinned at her had her toes curling against the floor. "Feel free to pressure me all you want." Then to her surprise, he scooped her up and basically raced up the stairs.

Instead of heading to the guest room she normally stayed in, he went to the one he'd moved to—with a king-sized bed.

After he set her down on the edge of the bed, he sat next to her, suddenly hands off. "I'm not expecting anything.... I like kissing you. I like you, Berlin. I think this could be—"

At his words, panic exploded inside her. She knew what it was, a bunch of deep-seated baggage from her childhood. Didn't make it any less terrifying and she couldn't let him finish his statement, couldn't risk he was going to ask for more.

"I like you too," she blurted. "But this is just...fun, okay? Nothing serious. We've got too much going on," she added at the hurt that flickered in his dark eyes. God, she was such a liar and the queen of self-sabotaging when something seemed to be too good.

And usually it was spot-on, because if it seemed too good, it often was. She was too afraid to hope that Chance fell into the actually good category, so she was going to play this safe.

She couldn't tell what he thought of her words, but he leaned in close, brushed his mouth over hers, then nipped her bottom lip. "If you say stop, we stop, okay?"

"Same goes for you."

"I'm not going to want to stop." His words were a wicked rumble that spiraled through her, warming her from the inside out.

This man completely unnerved her. From the moment she'd sorta stalked him and put a face to the man she'd been gaming with for years, she'd been smitten.

He kissed her again, more heated than before, with way more intent. This wasn't a teasing, slow kiss, but one of a man who was going for what he wanted.

She thought about pushing him back, straddling him, but he'd already taken over, had her pinned beneath him on the soft bed as he practically devoured her.

She arched up into him, wanting all that he had to offer. Spreading her thighs, she wrapped her legs around his waist as he rolled his hips against hers. Feeling bold by his very clear reaction, she reached between their bodies and palmed his erection over his jeans.

He groaned against her mouth, his breathing unsteady as he pulled back with clear effort. "It's been a while for me."

She squeezed his hard length gently.

And he groaned again even as he grasped her wrist. "I'm not coming in my pants."

She grinned now but sucked in a breath as he kissed her again, and she realized she could get used to this. God, she'd never thought much about kissing before but the way he did it with his whole being, the way he practically worshipped her mouth made her wonder if he'd show the same effort everywhere else.

As if he read her mind, he slid his hand under her T-shirt, his callused palms gliding up her waist. "Can I take this off?"

"Yes...you can take everything off." She was all in for this today. She'd never wanted anyone the way she was desperate for him. And getting naked now seemed like a really good idea.

Taking her at her word, he stripped off her shirt, his eyes going dark and hungry when he saw that she wasn't wearing a bra. Her nipples hardened under his heated gaze, and when he dipped his head to her breast, heat coiled low in her core, flared out in every direction.

He took his time working her up until she was a mass of exposed nerves—and then he moved lower. "Is this okay?" His voice was pitched low as he tugged her pants and panties off.

"I think you can assume anything you do is okay at this point."

He let out a surprised laugh, but just as quickly that hunger was back on his face as he spread her thighs. She was suddenly very aware of just how vulnerable she was, but the way he was looking down at her, as if he wanted to worship her...that was some kind of power.

If someone could bottle up this feeling and sell it, they'd be set for life.

She rolled her hips up slightly, knowing she was being demanding and not caring.

He met her gaze as he reached between her legs then stroked a gentle finger along her slick folds. He barely touched her, but it was as if he'd set something off inside her with his touch.

Her inner walls tightened at that stroke, the need to have him inside her overwhelming. Because she wanted more than his finger. She wanted all of him. "Please do something," she finally growled.

"Why am I not surprised by how impatient you are?" he asked even as he slid a thick finger inside her.

Her hips jolted off the bed at the welcome intrusion and then he dipped his head between her legs and she forgot about everything else as he stroked and teased her until she was needy and desperate and would have likely given him anything he asked for. Want her to hack the Pentagon? No problem.

She just needed the orgasm she could feel right on the horizon, just peeking up... "I'm so close." So close it bordered on painful.

He slid another finger inside her as he sucked on her clit, and that gave her exactly what she'd been chasing. Pleasure punched through her as he continued stroking his fingers in a steady rhythm, heightening her pleasure even more.

She came against his face, not caring about how loud she was being as another tremor shook her, the orgasm seeming to go on forever until all she could do was blink up at him. If he could do that with his fingers...

Giving her a lazy smile, he stretched out next to her and kissed her again, the taste of her still on him. She wasn't sure why she liked that so much, but she loved how raw he was. He didn't seem to hold anything back.

And she wanted to give him as much pleasure as he'd given her. So she reached between their bodies as he continued that slow exploration of her mouth, popped his button free.

But he placed his hand over hers, stilling her. "I realized I forgot about condoms earlier, but I don't care. I wanted you to come—I've been dying to taste you. We don't have to do anything else."

Well, his thick erection said otherwise. "There should be some in the bedside drawer," she whispered. "They keep these rooms stocked." Because so many of their crew crashed at the safe house, and for people who were hiding out.

He paused, all the muscles in his arms going tight as he pushed up. With the sunlight streaming in from the cracked blinds behind him, it illuminated his expression as her words registered.

He moved quickly, letting out a satisfied growl as he tugged one of the drawers open. Then he tossed a handful onto the bed before he stripped off his shirt.

She wanted to take over, to slowly undress him, but as she tracked his movements, was glad he was taking the initiative because she got to watch as he revealed every delicious inch of his hard body.

Moving onto her knees, she reached for him as he shucked the rest of his clothes, kicking his jeans away. "You're like a work of art," she whispered, drinking in all his hard lines and striations.

And to her surprise, his cheeks flushed the faintest shade of pink. For some reason that made her like him even more. How could he not be used to these kinds of compliments when he was built like this? Though it was clear he worked for it.

She stroked her fingers up his abdomen, chest, and trailed them down his biceps and forearms, shuddering at all that raw strength. "Seriously, you're incredible."

He made a sort of growling sound and took over again, pinning her beneath him so that they were skin to skin. She savored the feel of her nipples rubbing against his chest, the feel of his thick erection against her abdomen as he once again took his time kissing her.

But she had no patience, even after that orgasm, so she grasped his hard length and stroked once, slowly, enjoying how thick and heavy he was and imagining what he'd feel like inside her.

He groaned into her mouth, his entire body trembling at her touch. And yep, that was the kind of power she could get drunk on.

She was aware of him slapping out at the bed and it took a moment to realize he was reaching for one of the condoms. She made a move to grab it but he ripped it open and was rolling it over his impressive length before she could protest.

She raked her fingernails over his lower abdomen, grinned as his cock jumped, the condom shiny on that gorgeous display. "Art," she said, referring to her words earlier. Because everything about him was pure art.

He shook his head slightly. "You're good for my ego," he murmured as he covered her once again.

But this time he angled his erection between her thighs, teasing her already slick entrance as his mouth sought hers.

As he slid inside her, she bit his bottom lip, moaning at the way he stretched her until she knew she could come again. Because sweet baby pandas, this man was everything.

Even as she told herself that this was casual, that they'd just be friends, she was already mourning the time when this was over. Because she didn't want casual. She wanted to lock this man down, to keep him forever.

Aaaaand at that insane thought, she grasped onto his backside and urged him to move. Because she couldn't let her thoughts run away with her, couldn't start thinking of a future or anything past today.

Luckily he didn't need much urging and started moving inside her with long, hard strokes that had her body primed again, ready for another climax. Something that normally took a little time, but she'd also never wanted anyone like this. Had never felt so connected to someone like she did with him.

She didn't think it was going to take him long, not with the desperate sounds he was making. Sounds that were like actual music because, oh my god, he was into her as much as she was into him.

"I'm going to come again," she rasped out between kisses, digging her fingers into his ass as she urged him to move faster.

His response was more of a strangled sound than anything else, but he reached between their bodies and began teasing her clit—and set her off again.

The orgasm that had been on the periphery slammed into her. With each deep thrust and the combined stroking of her clit, it was too much. She couldn't get out any words as her climax crested higher, higher and then he was coming with her.

"God," was all he managed, which was more than her, as he nipped the sensitive spot on her shoulder, sending her into even more of a tailspin underneath him.

She lost all sense of time as pleasure continued to spiral through her, until he blinked down at her, his expression as sated as she assumed hers was.

"Are you hungry?" she whispered.

He blinked again even as he eased out of her, tugged the condom off.

"I need food." She sat up, still a little wobbly. But she had to get some distance between them in case he wanted to cuddle. Because then she'd be lost for good and give in to everything she wanted.

Which was him—specifically, imagining a future with him.

But he moved fast, snaking his arm around her waist and pulling her back on top of him as he dropped the condom...who knew where. "You're not running," he growled, burying his face against her neck as he pulled her flush against him again.

"No one's running."

"Liar." He nipped her neck again, sending another shiver through her.

How did he see right through her? "Just...hungry," she rasped out as he cupped one of her breasts.

"Yeah well so am I." Then he flipped her on her back and went down on her again.

She'd thought for sure they were done, but clearly he had other plans. And...oh. Oooh, god, this man was like quicksand and she was going to get sucked under if she wasn't careful.

But as he used that wicked, wonderful tongue on her again, it was hard to care.

CHAPTER 23

"I don't like this," Rowan grumbled from the driver's seat of the SUV. He'd been a surly teddy bear all morning since Berlin and Adalyn had come up with the perfect plan for getting pictures of the Acton brothers.

Berlin shot Adalyn a look, eyebrows raised. Adalyn simply shook her head and Berlin was pretty sure her boss and friend barely restrained an eye roll.

Then Chance turned around from the passenger seat to look at both of them, but his gaze remained on Berlin, his eyes flickering to the decent amount of cleavage she was showing off for just a moment. "I don't either."

"You two are being ridiculous," Adalyn responded before Berlin could. "And if I didn't know any better, I'd think this was a sexist thing."

Rowan turned around whip-fast. "Seriously?"

"No, I just like getting you riled up. But maybe this one is feeling sexist." She chin nodded at Chance.

Who simply shot her a dry look before his attention was once again on Berlin and her short blonde bob and sparkly pink dress. "We don't know enough about this crew, and one night of research doesn't feel like enough to drop into this place to get pictures of these assholes—if they're even there."

"The only way we're going to get more on this elusive gang is from this. And it's a good plan," Berlin said. "And we've already been over everything a billion times."

She'd been following multiple conversations on TikTok thanks to the information Eugene had given her, and they were relatively certain that the Acton brothers owned a tattoo parlor in New Orleans. She didn't think the city was a big hub for them, but a tattoo parlor would be a good place to conduct business and handle various amounts of cash. And the place was open late, which matched the kind of businesses their clientele would deal with. Not to mention it wouldn't be strange for different faces to move in and out, so for anyone watching the place it would be difficult to decipher who might be part of their operation or who was just a customer.

Overall, it was a really smart cover and one of the most common types of places for laundering money—which they were also likely doing. Berlin had tried hacking their cameras but couldn't lock into anything, which was interesting all by itself. She knew that these Acton brothers didn't like technology so maybe they didn't have cameras, but used actual people for security. Or maybe it was more localized and not connected to a bigger service.

Regardless, she and Adalyn were going inside to scope out the place—and get pictures. Because that was what Berlin needed. Once she had faces, she could get names. And from there, it was only a matter of time before she could do a deep dive on these operators. Because no matter how good anyone thought they were, they almost always left a trail.

"We've been over it twice," Chance grumbled before turning around—but not before sharing a look with Rowan.

Because apparently the two of them were friends now.

"I just don't like you going in there unarmed." Rowan turned around again. "And I get that you're a weapon, Adalyn, but I don't have to like it."

"I know," Adalyn said. "But we've got this and you'll see what we see. If anything is off, just bust in there."

"Oh we will." This was from Chance, who didn't turn around again but stared stonily out the front.

Which was probably the best for Berlin's sanity. After yesterday afternoon, then into the evening, then again this morning... Her entire body was weak. In the best way possible, but the only breaks she'd taken had been to eat, shower—though that had been with Chance too—and work online to track these guys down.

She slid on her fake glasses that would take images of everything inside the tattoo parlor. Everything she saw, her sparkly pink glasses would capture.

"Let's go." Adalyn slid out without waiting.

Berlin did the same, following along with Adalyn who was dressed differently than her. Instead of going for the bubblegum Barbie look, she was in all black, looking a lot like Berlin did normally. But she had on a wig as well, a light brunette one with soft curls and bangs that did a good job of covering her face.

The walk to get to the tattoo place took about ten minutes with the uneven sidewalks and city streets, but they hadn't been willing to risk parking closer. They were simply two tourists in town for the weekend, visiting from Biloxi.

The pink and orange neon *OPEN* sign was on so Adalyn opened the door for Berlin, moving in with her as if they were together. She slung her arm around Berlin's shoulders, her expression a scowl as they approached the front countertop.

In contrast, Berlin was all smiles to match her bubblegum outfit. This whole thing had been Adalyn's idea and she didn't hate the cover. Especially since Chance's tongue had basically fallen out of his mouth when she'd walked downstairs dressed in practically nothing.

There was one man behind the counter, two people sitting in the waiting area, and behind them, three glass windows showed people getting tattoos. They were all on display like fish in an aquarium.

"How can I help you?" the man asked, his gaze doing a slow once-over of Adalyn, not even acknowledging Berlin.

She tried not to let her ego be dented too much.

"My girl wants a tattoo. It's going to be her first and you guys have a good reputation." Which was actually true—they had tens of thousands of positive online reviews. Real ones too, not bots.

"Normally we have a four month wait, but you're in luck." His gaze was still on Adalyn as he shoved his long-sleeved shirt up to reveal inked sleeves of exquisite work. "We had three cancellations today. Mercury in retrograde or something." The guy shook his head slightly, clearly annoyed, before he smiled at Adalyn again. "Are you getting one today because I'd love to get my hands on you."

Okay, they might not be a real couple, but this guy didn't know that and he was putting on the flirt vibe hard. Also, gross.

"Just my girl." Adalyn's words were hard, clipped, which apparently didn't matter to the guy because he simply grinned at her. Apparently he had a death wish.

Berlin popped a piece of gum in her mouth and looked down at the glass countertop. "Ooh, that's pretty. Can you pull out some of those drawings?" She was looking down at his hands and arms, making sure she got a great view of his ink for the cameras. She could run them through various programs later, including NCIC, see if she got a hit on any of them. Luckily when people were booked for crimes, often (if the arresting officer wasn't lazy) distinguishing tattoos or markings were recorded.

"Maybe later you and your girl want to hang with me and my boys," he continued even as he pulled out the pages of drawings for Berlin. "I love an older woman."

"But I don't like little boys." Adalyn's voice was saccharine sweet. "Come on, let's get out of here—"

"I'm just messing with you—unless you do want to hang out. But stay, let your girl pick out something fun. So where are you thinking of getting your ink, sweetheart?" Now he looked at Berlin, but his gaze strayed to her breasts. Stayed there. Couldn't even be bothered to look just a little higher at her face.

Yep, gross.

"Inner thigh, probably. Where's your restroom?"

He cleared his throat, jerked his thumb toward a hallway lined with different illustrations as he leaned over the countertop to talk to Adalyn.

The last thing Berlin heard was, "Do you ever bring a third into the bedroom?"

Jesus, this guy wasn't even kind of subtle. As she made her way down the hallway, she slowed, looked at the art, but was mostly scanning for any hidden cameras. Instead of opening the bathroom door, which was clearly marked, she opened a door that should lead to one of the tattoo rooms.

There were two guys in there—one giving a tattoo to another. Out of the corner of her eyes, she could see Adalyn through the glass keeping the other guy's attention. "Oh, sorry, I was just looking for the bathroom. Oooh, that's cool. And so big. Does it hurt?" She leaned into the Barbie persona, smacking her gum, pitching her voice a little higher.

"You're not supposed to be in here." The bearded tattoo artist with ink all up his left arm and on his knuckles didn't look up.

"It's fine, you can stay and watch if you want." The guy in the chair was about forty, with a trim beard and a sculpted jaw. Potentially Mediterranean heritage. He might be considered conventionally attractive if not for the scar that started under one of his ears and dipped low under his black Henley.

Berlin grinned, sauntering into the room, her pink heels clicking on the tile as she swept her gaze over everything in interest before turning it back onto the two men. "Thanks. My girlfriend brought me to get a tattoo but I'm not sure what I want yet."

The guy's gaze flicked past her, likely sizing up Berlin. But his mouth curved up. "I see she's shooting down Luis."

Berlin shrugged. "Maybe, maybe not."

The tattoo artist looked up then and she captured his face with her glasses as he glanced at her. He did the same sweep over her, but it was mostly with disinterest until he reached her feet. "Nice shoes."

"Thanks. So how long have you been doing this?"

He just shrugged.

"Santi isn't much of a talker," the man on the chair murmured, his gaze amused.

"What about you? Are you a talker?" Berlin asked.

He just shrugged, but he was watching her with some amusement. "Depends."

"I'm Kitty by the way," she said, hoping he'd tell her his name, fake or not. Sometimes aliases could help as much as real names when researching. She moved closer to the artist, leaned over slightly to glance at his work—and intentionally showing off her cleavage. Guys could be so stupid sometimes and she wasn't above using her assets to get information.

"You're in my light." The tattoo artist was all growly, but there was no real bite to his words.

"Stop being a dick. And I'm Carlos," the guy murmured as he let his head fall back, his eyes closing with a sigh.

Berlin moved out of the way. She'd just about overstayed her welcome and she'd gotten what she came for anyway—multiple angles of their faces and clean images of their ears. "Sorry, I'll leave you guys alone. I've gotta pee anyway. Thanks for letting me check out your work."

"I didn't let you do anything, you just barged in here," the man named Santi muttered.

Smothering a smile, she hurried out, went to the restroom, which had more art, pretended to take care of business, then washed her hands and met Adalyn back in the waiting room.

"Have you decided what you want yet?" Adalyn's voice was bored as she tucked Berlin up against her.

"I think I want to wait. It looks too painful," she whined. "And I only like pain if there's a payoff," she added playfully. In return, Adalyn gave her an indulgent smile. Man, she really was good at acting. "Besides, that guy back there was kinda grumpy. Maybe we should try somewhere else."

"You're not supposed to be back in the rooms," the man who she now knew was potentially named Luis practically whined. "I'm gonna get bitched at later."

Berlin popped a bubble of her gum at him in response. *Boo freaking hoo.*

Adalyn gave him a once-over. "We might be back later if she changes her mind."

"Even if you don't, feel free to hit me up anytime." He slid a card across the countertop to Adalyn. "My boys and I are partying later tonight."

Berlin snatched up the card and tucked it in the V of her sparkly dress. "You don't get to hit on my woman right in front of me. It's disrespectful."

He actually looked at her now, as if she hadn't been there the whole time, and held up his palms slightly. "Sorry, sweetheart, no offense."

"You've been propositioning my girlfriend from the moment we walked in here and you mean no offense?" She leaned in, really liking this role.

"Just don't be surprised if you leave work one day and your bike's on fire." There were a handful of motorcycles in the parking lot so she took a gamble that one of them was his.

His eyes widened as she swiveled and stomped off as Adalyn murmured, "My kitty's got claws."

Once they were outside, Adalyn snickered.

"Threatening arson was a nice touch."

"He was rude." She slid her hand into Adalyn's, linking her fingers with hers as they headed down the sidewalk. She seriously doubted they'd be followed, but they'd planned ahead of time to have a normal day of shopping and sightseeing after stopping in the tattoo parlor.

Just in case.

If someone was following them, they watched Adalyn and Berlin buy fancy chocolates, even fancier lingerie, stop for mimosas at an open bar, a little boutique where Adalyn bought her a couple dresses, and then they disappeared into a shopping center. From there, they dipped into different dressing rooms, completely changed their appearances and then left via a back exit.

"You weren't followed," Rowan said as they shut the SUV doors behind them.

"How did the pictures look?" Berlin asked as Rowan pulled away from the curb.

"Not bad. You got a lot of images," Chance said, handing her the tablet. "I went through some of them and the angles are all really good."

Shivers rolled through her as their fingers brushed and she did not imagine the heated look he gave her.

Ignoring it for now—or pretending to—she snagged all the facial images she'd captured and uploaded them into multiple programs—some she'd hacked into and some she or her friend Gage had created. Once she'd done that, she pulled out the card the guy had given to Adalyn and input that phone number as well. It was going to be a lot of work cross-referencing incoming and outgoing phone numbers, so she pinged her friend and sometimes coworker Hailey with all the pertinent info. Because she needed more sets of eyes on this. She thought about asking Gage for help, but his wife Nova was currently on bed rest in her ninth month of pregnancy and she didn't want to bother either of them.

Then she texted Hazel, just letting the special agent know that she was working on finding the Acton brothers. She didn't have to check in, but Berlin believed in keeping open communication, especially since the other woman had gone out on a limb and given her information she hadn't needed to. Of course, Redemption Harbor Security had gotten the FBI a couple wins recently, but still.

She got a thumbs-up from Hazel.

"Luis is going to be disappointed you're not calling him," Rowan grumbled from the front seat.

Berlin looked up for the first time since the guys had picked them up, realized they were almost to the safe house. "You can't actually be jealous of that guy," Berlin said, snickering.

Rowan just shrugged. "Not jealous. Just didn't like the way he was watching my wife."

Berlin shot Adalyn a sideways glance and the other woman just shook her head. Before meeting Chance, Berlin couldn't have imagined that she'd like a man getting jealous like that. But...she didn't think she'd hate it if Chance had the same reaction to her.

And that terrified her. She hadn't seen him coming, had never expected anything like this with him. Now...she wasn't sure what to think about anything.

CHAPTER 24

*The best thing that ever happened to me is
you.*

"This is pretty interesting," Berlin murmured, seemingly more to herself than Chance as he stepped into the living room where she was stretched out on one of the couches. In little shorts that showed off toned legs and a tiny tank top, she looked good enough to eat.

"What is?" He met her gaze when he wanted to drink in all the soft lines of her. They'd been back at the safe house for a few hours, and he felt like they were in a waiting pattern. Not that he wasn't grateful for all their help, but he was starting to go stir-crazy.

She blinked and looked up at him. "What? Oh...nothing. I've just been going over all the incoming and outgoing calls to that guy Luis's phone. His real name too. But he's got some shady contacts... What's that?"

"Food. You need to eat something." He sat on the couch next to her, handed her a four-cheese grilled sandwich. "I've also got soup for you in the kitchen because I wasn't sure you'd want to eat that in here."

"You cooked for me?" There was a slightest accusatory note in her voice, even if she was smiling at him.

"It's grilled cheese and tomato soup."

"It's my favorite comfort food."

"I remember you saying that."

"Oh right... Sometimes I forget how much I told you."

He held out a hand and pulled her to her feet. "Come on. You can bring your laptop with you, but you still need to eat. You'll feel better once you do."

"Thank you for this." The way she looked at him, as if he'd hung the moon... He could get used to that.

He shrugged. "It's the least I can do. And for the record, if you need me to do more...I'm here. I can't hack like you, but I'm decent enough with research."

"There are actually some things you can look over. It'll help speed things up."

"Good," he said as she sat and he started ladling soup into a bowl for her. "So what's interesting about Luis's phone records?"

"One pattern sticks out, but only because of the weird consistency of the calls. Every Sunday at five a.m., he gets a call that lasts for approximately twenty seconds. It could be nothing, but it's so damn consistent."

"Same number?"

"No, each one is a burner, which makes sense for guys doing illegal things. I'm now running all the burner numbers but doubt I'll get anything."

"Did you get anything on the images from the tattoo parlor?"

"The guy named Carlos is a ghost. I know I said everyone leaves a trail, but I'm coming up with *nothing* on him. Santi, aka Santiago Alonso, is a tattoo artist, from New Orleans, and started working at the shop two years ago. I can't tell if he's dirty or not or just working for assholes. Or maybe...I don't know."

He nudged her laptop out of the way as he sat next to her. "You're incredible, and if anyone is going to find anything, it's you."

"Don't put too much faith in me," she muttered.

"Why not? You're amazing." And he had a feeling that she didn't hear it enough. Anytime he complimented her, she didn't seem to know how to react.

She gave him a jerky shrug, then averted her gaze as she focused on her soup.

He'd also realized last night, after the first time they'd gotten naked together, that she was a runner. It had been so damn clear in her body language that she was trying to "wham, bam, thank you ma'am" and run.

But he wasn't having that. When he'd first met her in person, he'd had a fairly clear plan that he was going to ditch her help and do this on his own. Then he'd been determined to keep his distance.

After having a taste of her... Yeah, there was no going back. He was addicted and he wasn't going to run from Berlin. Run *after* her maybe, but not run from her.

"If I can't find him, I don't want you to hate me," she whispered, looking up with big, blue-green eyes that he could drown in.

Her words surprised him. Or more, the intensity behind them did.

Setting his spoon down, he reached for her free hand. "First, I could never hate you. You've gone out of your way to help me, a stranger—"

"You're not a stranger," she murmured.

"Fine, not a stranger. But you're doing a lot more than anyone else would have done and...I'm incredibly grateful. And I'm going to keep calling you incredible, because you are."

"You're pretty incredible yourself." Her cheeks flushed pink as she spoke.

And he realized she was talking about something totally different now. He grinned slightly. "You tried to run from me."

"I didn't run." She picked up her spoon, ignoring his gaze again.

"You did. And for the record, if you try to run in the future, I'll just follow." She spent all her time taking care of all the people in her life and he was starting to realize that no one took care of her. That was changing—he wanted to be the one who took care of her now. Though if he came out and said that, it'd terrify her even more. Still, he wanted to make one thing clear: she could run, but she couldn't hide.

She looked over at him with an expression he couldn't begin to read. Which was fine, because he didn't need a response. He just wanted her to know where he stood.

By her side.

***

"I'm gonna grab this," Chance murmured, standing and stretching. He'd been looking over the file she'd sent him for the last hour, but paused when he saw Evander's name on the caller ID. It wasn't like Hot Shot to call so quickly after just calling less than a week ago.

Berlin gave him a distracted smile and nodded as she continued working.

"Hey, everything okay?" he asked as he headed up the stairs.

"Yeah, just checking in."

"Checking in or checking up on me?"

Evan laughed lightly. "Both. What's going on with your girl who's not really your girl?"

"We're making progress."

"On what? Seriously, what's this all about? You had me do a deep dive on someone I can barely get any information on and then I hear nothing from you."

He eased the bedroom door shut behind him, sank onto the end of the bed. The room smelled like her, like *them*, and he inhaled deeply. "Enzo's missing and she's helping me find him."

Evan was quiet for a long moment. "I thought you guys weren't talking."

"We weren't. Then we started again and...Enzo's involved in some bad stuff and my girl has resources I don't."

"Your girl, huh?"

"Shut up."

"You sure you can trust her? You just met her."

"I didn't just meet her. We've been gaming together for years. I just...didn't know she was a woman."

"Wait, is this Moonlighter? The trash talk king?"

Chance snickered. "Yeah."

"Trash talk queen, then. So, you sure you can trust her?"

"With my life, no questions asked."

"Oh. Shit."

"Yeah." He scrubbed a hand over his face. "She's brilliant. But I don't know if it's going to be enough—hey, oh shit, Enzo's calling. I gotta go." He ended the call without waiting for a response to switch over. "Hey, you okay? Where are you?"

"I'm fine. But I know I fell off communication and things were...rough between us. I didn't want you to think I was ghosting you. I can't talk long, but I just wanted to let you know I'm okay and I'll be going offline again for a bit. And...I love you. I don't think I ever said that enough, or at all, when we were kids. But you did a lot for us. For Ivy, for me. You kept it together when Mom went off the rails, and had way too much responsibility... Thank you."

"Enzo—" But the line had gone dead. He cursed even as he dialed him back, but it went straight to voicemail. It went to voicemail again as he hurried down the stairs where he found Berlin already off the couch, her laptop tucked under her arm.

"Your brother called you," she said before he could say a word. "I've been monitoring his phone from the moment you told me everything. And if I have, chances are the people he stole from have been too. I've found him—and we need to go now."

Ice slid through his veins as the truth of her words hit him square in the chest. "We've got to go."

CHAPTER 25

"Holy shit," Chance murmured, as he took the exit Berlin motioned to.

"What? Are we being tailed?" She didn't turn around in her seat, but he watched as she glanced in the sideview mirror.

"No. I don't think so anyway. But I think I know where Enzo is." They'd been driving north for a few hours to the last known destination of Enzo's phone.

Berlin had worked her magic and narrowed it down within a mile. She said under other circumstances it would have been closer, but Enzo's phone call had pinged off one of the few towers in the area. "According to this, he called from outside this small diner." She pointed to it on the map without touching her screen.

"I know. But he won't still be there, if he ever was." They'd just been driving in this direction in the hopes they'd figure out something once they got closer. "Growing up, we had a very distant cousin through marriage who had a cabin out here. But not in Louisiana. Across the state border in Natchez."

"You think there's a chance he's in Natchez, then?"

"My brother is really stupid sometimes but he's also really smart. He kept that call with me short, likely thinking it couldn't be traced."

"Which is just movie crap, not reality." Berlin sniffed indignantly.

Chance cleared his throat. "If I had to bet, I'd say he drove over into Louisiana to make the call. We went to that cabin outside Natchez proper a few times. It's in a rural area and isolated on a lake. If he was going to hide out somewhere, it might be in that area." Something Chance wouldn't have ever thought of, but seeing where Enzo had called from...it made sense.

"Well, it's literally only a six-minute drive into Natchez. And you know your brother. That diner closed at three anyway so it's not like it's open and I can't imagine him calling you then sitting there the last few hours. Do you remember the address?"

"No, but my cousin's name was Danny Marceaux. His parents were Uncle Danny and Aunt Alice. Ah, same last name."

She was mostly quiet as she worked, pulling up property records from what he glanced at. "You still talk to your cousin?"

"No, but Enzo might. When...Ivy, my sister, died, my mom went off the deep end. Looking back, I don't blame her. The grief was too much for her to bear." His throat grew tight, but he pushed the words out. "She lashed out at that side of the family, blaming everyone for not giving us enough money to save her. But it wasn't their fault. It wasn't anyone's fault. Other than corporate greed," he muttered. They'd been too poor to pay for her treatment, so his mom had asked everyone she knew for money. Everyone had pitched in, but it hadn't been enough. After Ivy had died, their mom might as well have died too. "In her anger, she pushed everyone away until she literally ran away."

"I'm really sorry," Berlin murmured. "And I found the property. They sold the cabin to your cousin about a decade ago, and from what I can tell, he's turned it into a rental. Place is nice too." She twisted the screen so he could look.

"That's not like the cabin I remember."

"According to these very helpful reviews and all these pictures from rental sites, we've got a pretty decent layout of this place and property." She jumped slightly as thunder rumbled overhead.

They'd been driving right into a storm for the last hour and he knew that soon it would break wide open on them.

She plugged the address in and he realized they were only twenty minutes away. As they headed down the two-lane highway, her phone rang into the relative quiet.

"Hey, Adalyn, you're on speaker," Berlin said as her phone connected to the SUV's Bluetooth.

"Any progress?" Adalyn jumped right into it.

"Yeah, I think we've found the location. We're not far out. I've just sent you the possible coordinates and I'll let you know if he's there once we get there. Where are you guys?"

"In the air, headed your way."

Chance knew that Adalyn had her pilot's license and the four of them had taken a short trip over to Fairhope, Alabama for reasons they hadn't seen fit to tell him.

"There's a storm rolling in," Berlin said even as the first few raindrops splashed on the SUV's windshield.

"We're flying right into it," Adalyn muttered. "We're not there yet, but we might have to land before we make it to you guys."

"It's fine, we're just going to touch base with his brother and figure out what's going on."

"Chance," Adalyn said, apparently ignoring Berlin, "can you keep her out of trouble?"

Berlin snarled. "I swear to god—"

"Yep," Chance said. "I'll make sure she hangs back until I scope things out."

"All right. I would tell you guys to wait for us, but I know that's not going to happen. So just be smart and stay safe until we catch up with you." Then she disconnected before Berlin could respond.

"I'm not leaving you behind," Chance said when it was clear that Berlin had worked up a head of steam at Adalyn's words.

She blinked. "Oh. You lied to her?"

"She's not my boss. And you're my friend." He shrugged.

"But? Because I know there's a but just hanging out, waiting for you to drop it."

He snorted softly. "Fine. With all your skills, can you hack into that security system I saw in some of the pictures?" He nodded at her laptop. "Or the cameras?"

She grinned, her expression practically feral. "Oh yeah. But only once we're closer."

"Good. I'll need you to act as my eyes as I infiltrate. And before you argue, it makes more sense for you to hang back only so you can guide me. I need your help and I don't want to go in blind." Because there was no way in hell he was letting her go into an unknown situation with him, especially with a clear threat hanging in the air. For all they knew, the Acton brothers could have figured out where Enzo was.

"I'm well aware that you're handling me right now," she muttered.

"Is it working?"

"Only because you're right and it makes more sense for me to be your eyes. Won't do any good for both of us to get caught. Or worse." She bit her bottom lip for a long moment. "I'll do what I do best. I'll be your backup."

"Thank you." That was one thing he didn't have to worry about now. Because he couldn't go in after his brother if he was worried about Berlin's safety. He cared more for her than he'd ever cared for anyone. So much so, it was something he couldn't dwell on, or he'd pull a U-turn and put miles between Berlin and any upcoming danger.

CHaPTer 26

Rain pelted the SUV's windshield in sheets as Chance and Berlin sat in the parked vehicle. He'd pulled over once they were about two miles from the cabin and had turned off the windshield wipers as he looked over the images Berlin had pulled up, including a very helpful aerial shot from one of the rental sites.

"What's the closest house to this cabin?"

"Another cabin across the lake, about eight miles west. It's a hike. We're currently on your cousin's property and it stretches out to the west for about an acre and a half. In the direction you'll be heading, you'll run into his place before crossing over into any other property." She shifted the map slightly. "And that's not for almost seven miles east. There shouldn't be any neighbors nearby. And the house to the east is a hunting cabin anyway so it should be empty."

"Okay, I'll keep my eyes and ears on for you," he said, motioning to the small camera he'd pinned to his shirt and then to his Bluetooth. "Should I tuck the camera under my rain jacket?"

"It's waterproof. I mean, don't soak it, but it should be fine." She glanced out the window, frowned. "Maybe tuck it under your jacket, but don't forget to bring it out again. I don't like not going with you," she grumbled as she turned back to him.

"Do you always go with your crew?"

"No. But it's just the two of us. And I'm worried about you," she blurted.

"I'm worried about you too. I hate leaving you here, but it makes the most sense for the mission." And he knew she'd be safer here hidden in the woods miles from the cabin, something he kept to himself. He simply couldn't have her running headfirst into danger.

"Be safe. I don't...want to lose you," she whispered.

Her barely admitted words hit him right in the chest. "You're not going to lose me. If Enzo's here, I'm getting him out. I'll convince him to come with us and regroup. No matter what he's taken, maybe we can figure out a deal with those psychos or get him to relocate somewhere." It would have to be under another name, but these were things Chance had been thinking about the entire drive here. No matter what, he was going to keep his brother safe.

Leaning over, he brushed his lips over Berlin's, the kiss turning deeper until he forced himself to pull back. Without another word, he slipped out of the vehicle, the pounding of rain increasing the moment he opened the door.

Pulling the jacket hood over his face, he stalked through the woods, his all-weather boots perfect for this trek.

"Can you hear me?" Berlin asked in his ear.

"Copy, loud and clear." He squinted against the rain as he shoved the frond of a cinnamon fern out of his way.

His boots sank deeper and deeper the farther he made it toward the lake and cabin. For the most part it was just pine and oak trees with some random foliage mixed in. By the time he started seeing clusters of American beautyberry bushes, he knew he was close.

"You were right," he murmured, though no one would be able to hear him over the torrent of rain.

"I'm always right. But about what?" Berlin asked, her voice quieter than normal over the line because of the rain.

"The American beautyberries," he said. "There are a bunch of them on the edge of the woods and I can now just make out the cabin. There's a light on too." They were about half an hour to sunset, but the thunderstorm had blanketed the skies in dark gray so he was already moving around in shadows.

"Told you. It's amazing how much people share online. But I'm glad they do or my job would be a lot harder."

She'd created a full layout of the property based on images from reviewers, a newspaper write-up on rentals in the area, and from the actual rental site. And had told him that once he saw the bright clusters of purple berries, he should be close to the forest line and have a visual of the house.

"I'm also picking up a couple different signals. This is a smart house," she murmured, more to herself than him, he was certain. "Aannd you're clear to get inside," she said, five minutes later. "I unlocked a window on the west side of the house. Should be a bathroom."

"Thanks. I'm going quiet now." He wouldn't say anything unless absolutely necessary.

After visually scanning for any traps or trip wires he made his way across the open space from the woods to the wide-open west side porch that surrounded the cabin. This place was a lot different from when he'd been a kid. Everything had been updated down to the new Hardie board exterior. It was new and fresh and the kind of place people would love to stay in to get away from crowds and relax.

When he approached the porch, he paused at the cans hooked up on a long fishing wire. "See that?" he whispered.

"Yeah. Crude, but effective. I can't pick up any interior cameras, but I've made it so that you're invisible to the outside ones. Can you avoid the wire?"

"Yeah." Slowly, he scanned the length of the porch, saw that the wire ran along the entire thing. Since the house was up off the ground, likely because of potential flooding, he had to climb up one of the columns, then ease his body over the near invisible wire. If it wasn't for the rain leaving droplets splattered along it, glinting under the flashes of lightning, he might not have seen it.

His boots were quiet on the wooden porch.

"Be careful," Berlin whispered. "It's too damn quiet and I don't like that I can't see inside."

Yeah, he didn't like it either, but that was part of the job. He stripped off the wet jacket and all-weather heavy-duty waterproof pants Berlin had insisted he put on over his cargo pants. She hadn't been wrong either. Because now he could sneak into the house dry-ish and not worry about leaving a huge trail behind him.

Once he slipped through the window into what turned out to be a small bathroom with a toilet, sink and shower he wouldn't fit in, he withdrew his weapon and listened.

Rain pounded against the metal roof, making it impossible to hear much else. Which was good and bad for him. Though he hated trekking through the house in his wet boots, he wasn't going to take them off.

He eased the door open, weapon out, into a quiet hallway. The walls were painted a soft gray, with white beadboard on the bottom half. Two black-and-white pictures of the nearby lake were on the wall in front of him, a narrow table with six books in between fish-shaped bookends underneath them. One direction would lead to the front of the house, where according to the layout should be the foyer, then a set of stairs.

So he headed in the other direction toward what would be a living room and connected kitchen. As he made it to the end of the hallway, he froze at a clanging sound.

"Are you okay?" Berlin whispered, though no one would overhear her.

Chance didn't respond. Instead, he moved to the opposite wall on the hallway, trying to use the reflection from the bank of windows that ran down the entire back of the house. But curtains were drawn on all of them.

On the chance someone had heard him, he ducked low to avoid getting his head blown off and peered around the corner.

And froze.

There was a woman with her back to him at a stovetop, and soft classical music piping in from somewhere he couldn't see. His instinct was to lower the weapon, but he couldn't until he knew the situation.

When a man stepped into view, Chance moved out into the living room and raised his pistol—until his brother turned around.

Enzo's eyes widened, but he shoved the woman behind him as she let out a short scream. "What the hell!"

Chance lowered the weapon to the side, but didn't put it away fully. "Are you in danger? Who else is here?"

"I'm...in danger, yes, but not right this second. Nicola, this is my brother. He's not a danger to us."

A wide-eyed, dark-haired woman a solid foot shorter than his brother peeked around his back.

Chance sheathed his weapon as he stepped forward. "I don't think we have a lot of time, so I'm cutting through all the niceties. Did you steal drugs from the Acton brothers?"

"Are you seriously asking me that?" Enzo's eyes went flinty.

"I need to know what I'm up against. I can't believe you'd ever even run drugs... Oh my god," he trailed off, his gaze landing on the woman again. "You weren't running drugs. You were running..."

"I wasn't running people. Not intentionally. I was doing a favor for Brody Williams. I didn't realize it was for a bunch of psychos who wanted me to deliver a van full of women to some assholes in North Florida. So I ran with them, tried to stay off the grid. I had enough cash and reached out to Danny, asked him for help. I didn't give him specifics, so he has no clue what's going on, but he said I could use this place."

This changed everything. "A *van* full of women?"

"There's eight of us." The woman spoke quietly as she stepped out from behind his brother fully. She didn't have an accent either.

"Are you American?"

"Yeah."

"How old are you?" Unfortunately he had an understanding of how trafficking worked from some of his previous rescue missions and she was older than he normally saw.

The look she gave him was dry. "I'm twenty-eight, and yes, I know I'm not the normal age group. But I was taken for personal reasons." Her jaw clenched, rage flickering in her dark eyes for a moment.

"We need to get everyone out of here now. When you called me, my friend was able to track your call. And if she did, then anyone else tracking your phone was able to as well. But we headed here right away so if we leave now—"

"Chance, we've got company," Berlin's voice said into his earpiece. "Two SUVs just rolled by on the road, headed your way. You've got maybe six minutes, but they're booking it."

"Okay, change of plans. Get everyone in here, we've gotta go." He tapped his ear once as he moved fully into the kitchen. And that was when he saw that the woman was wearing a walking boot.

"What?" His brother stared at him, but the woman turned off the stove, clearly digesting everything faster.

"My friend has eyes on the road and two SUVs are headed this way. Any women in here, we need to move. They can't be trapped in this house." He knew from the online pictures that there was a boathouse and hopefully a kayak or two. "Get the women to the boathouse and I'm going to create a distraction."

Enzo pulled out a small radio and relayed a short message into it. Moments later, seven young women—or teens, he wasn't sure—raced into the kitchen. Most of them looked Latina, and if he had to guess they'd been trafficked from Mexico or Central America. His Spanish was rusty, but he said, "Bad men are on the way and if you want to survive, we have to leave out the back door now."

Enzo added, "Es mi hermano, confío en él."

They all nodded almost as one and fell in step, hurrying out the back sliding glass door. As soon as it opened, wind gusted in, sending the curtains flapping wildly.

"Go, go, go," he urged. "Can you carry her?" he asked Enzo.

"I can't leave you behind," his brother insisted. "This is my mess."

"This isn't a mess and I'm proud of you for this," he said even as he leaned down, pulled out another pistol and two loaded magazines, handed them to Enzo. "Get them out of here. Use kayaks or just swim, but get across the lake and out of sight. The rain will cover your movements. I'm going to do what I do best. Just trust me on this. Get to the other side and my friend will pick you up," he said, knowing Berlin would hear him. "Her people will help them, I swear, now go." He shoved his brother out the door even as he heard engines in the distance.

Enzo scooped up the American woman and disappeared into the blanket of falling rain.

Chance shut and locked the sliding door behind them. Then he turned the gas stovetop on, blew out the pilot lights. "You still with me, Berlin?"

"Of course. What do you need?"

"I want to get all of these assholes in here and take them out."

Chapter 27

"I don't like any of this," Berlin growled, but the lights in the house went dark around him. "Just get out of the damn house."

"I can't do that. I've gotta slow them down."

"You need backup."

"*You* are my backup," he snapped. "I'm on the second floor now, west side of the house. I can see...two SUVs parking. Eight tangos spilling out." He had to stay far away from the kitchen as he drew these monsters into this house.

They'd been trafficking women or at least worked with the people who were behind this. Considered these women "product" and he was pretty sure Brody Williams had known it. He had to have, and Chance was going to make sure he paid for that too. But that would be later.

"Can you see anything on the cameras?" he asked as he slid behind one of the open doorways of a bedroom. If these guys were like his former unit, or even remotely trained, they'd sweep rooms separately, then check in with each other.

"Yeah. Two of the men are moving toward the lake and they're out of my range." She let out a curse. "Okay, it's fine, we'll deal with that. Two are moving in toward the back, one is going in through the garage, another is using the same window you did and two...okay, they're at the front door. Weapons are out... They're shooting their way in."

A gas explosion rumbled the entire house, the ground shaking beneath him.

"Oh my god, the two men on the back porch just flew backward. They're... One is dead and the other won't make it. Everyone else has breached the house. I don't have eyes on them anymore, but the kitchen is on fire. I can see it through one of the outside cameras."

That sounded about right. "You can see where I am, right? With my tracker?"

"Yeah."

"Okay, set off any smart devices in the house, starting with the far east side. I want these guys spooked and off-kilter." He kept his voice pitched low as he heard faint movement down at the end of the hallway. "Start in thirty seconds. I've gotta go dark now." Not technically dark, but he wouldn't be able to talk after this.

"Okay. I've got you." She sounded like she was moving, but he couldn't tell and he had to trust she had this handled. The woman had hacked a satellite and tracked down his brother. She was incredible and he was thankful she was on his side.

Through the crack in the door, he saw an armed man in jungle-type fatigues, wearing a dark green helmet over a balaclava, step into a bathroom then come back out a couple moments later. Then he dipped into another room, was in there for a few long moments before he moved back out.

He continued in Chance's direction until he paused, slightly tilted his head as if listening to someone else. That was when Chance heard the whir of something metal in the distance, then water start to run.

"Halfway through clearing upstairs," the man said quietly in perfect

English. Then, "Okay." He turned, starting to head back the way he'd come, so Chance moved out into the hallway, whisper quiet.

The government had spent a lot of money training him, and as he slipped up behind the masked man he moved fast, grabbed the top of the helmet, yanked back to control the guy. Then he hit the man's carotid with his kukri, fast and hard, slicing deep.

The man jerked under the assault, his hands going up for an instant, but just as quickly his weapon thudded to the floor as blood arced out against the wall and nearby door.

Music blasted in the distance and he thought he heard the faint sound of gunfire, but couldn't be sure over the noise and rain still thundering against the roof. Even though it wouldn't hide him for long, he dragged the body into the nearby bathroom. Then, using the guy's own blood, he took the tango's limp hand, smeared it in the blood, then pressed perfect fingerprints into the side of the cabinet.

They might not need it but in case shit went sideways and these guys overran him, then cleaned up the bodies, he hoped Berlin and her people could use the prints to track them down later.

"One down," he whispered. Well, technically three. When Berlin didn't respond, his adrenaline spiked. "B?"

Nothing.

Now, fear, more than adrenaline, surged through him, but he forced it down as he pulled out the dead tango's earpiece, put it in his free ear.

Nothing from that end either, but if they communicated, he'd hear it.

"Charlie, check in." The new earpiece crackled to life as Chance hurried down the hallway, making his way to the stairs.

When no one responded, he figured Charlie was the guy he'd just killed.

"Charlie, check in now." A pause, then. "Everyone convene at meeting point three. "I found a surprise in the woods."

No. No, no, no. The only thing that could be a surprise was... Berlin. If they'd hurt her... He couldn't even go there.

As he reached the bottom of the stairs, the sink was running, lights from the living room were blinking on and off and Mozart's *The Marriage of Figaro* was blasting from unseen speakers. The sprinklers had come on, dousing most of the fire so that it hadn't spread, but now everything was soaked.

It was like a nightmare funhouse, with lightning flashing outside. Instead of heading straight out the back door, he made his way down the hallway to the foyer in the front—and dodged what would have been a deadly shot.

Plaster exploded behind him as a man jumped out at him from the living room, geared up the same as the dead guy upstairs. Fatigues, balaclava and a helmet, which seemed like overkill for bagging a bunch of helpless women and Enzo. This level of force didn't make sense, but he mentally shelved it as he struck out at the man, slamming the base of his palm in the guy's shoulder as he yanked his elbow, broke his weapon-toting arm.

The man let out a short scream before Chance shoved his blade up through his head, kicked him back.

One more down. Now he had to find Berlin.

CHAPTER 28

"You're a little older than we normally like, but you'll do well for us." A man wearing a dark mask and military-style fatigues grabbed Berlin's chin, turned her face back and forth as he inspected her, shined a flashlight in her face. As if she was a couch to be purchased.

Which to this asshole, she was.

Rage billowed up inside her as she squinted against the brightness, but she shoved it down. If she fought back against this monster, he'd take her out easily.

He'd come upon her in the woods when she'd been trying to reverse out of the SUV's hiding spot. But it had been stuck in thick mud so she'd gotten out and found herself staring down the barrel of a weapon. She hadn't even seen him moving up on her in the darkness. Even though she'd kept the headlights and interior lights off, he'd have seen the dashboard ones and heard the damn engine.

"Now tell me your name and what you're doing here." He peered into the tinted window, looking for what, she wasn't sure. "I know you're not alone."

"My name's Kitty. I'm staying across the lake and—"

Pain exploded in her cheek as he backhanded her so that she fell against the side of the SUV. At least it wasn't a direct punch, but it still stung.

"Lie again and you lose some teeth."

She winced slightly. "Fine," she gritted out as her cheekbone throbbed. "I'm Beatrice." A lie, but no one would make up a name like that and she had the fake ID to prove it. "An old friend of mine called me, asked for help with something. He said he needed to transport something and to bring an SUV. That's all I know." She kept eye contact like Skye had told her, weaving in enough truth with her lies that she'd sound believable.

"What's your friend's name?"

"Enzo."

Surprise flickered in his eyes, maybe because she'd been honest. "Hmm." Then his weapon hand wavered and she was pretty sure he thought about just shooting her right then and there. But he said, "Give me your keys now."

She shrugged and tossed them to him as rain continued to flood around them. For a moment she was tempted to run, but knew she wouldn't get far in what had turned into a boggy mess.

He ducked into the SUV, turned on the headlights, then looked at the vehicle registration, and her ID from her wallet, both of which had information listed for one Beatrice Smith. He also pulled out her phone, bashed it against the side of the door until it cracked before he tossed it into the mud. "You weren't lying," he murmured.

"I learn quickly."

He snorted softly. "For your sake I hope so." Then he motioned for her to step back. "Turn around, head that way. We're going to find your friend Enzo and see how much you're worth to him."

Well, crap on a cracker. Berlin just hoped Chance got to them first or she managed to figure a way out of this. Her boots weren't like Chance's and they got stuck every step she took, making the trek laborious. Her thighs trembled after a while as she struggled to pull her feet out of the muddy woods. The farther they made it from the SUV, the less the headlights illuminated their way as they plunged into real darkness.

"Jesus, can't you go any faster?" the man snarled, pushing her.

She cried out in surprise as she fell face first in the mud. Something pierced her left shoulder, but she bit back another cry as he yanked her to her feet. "I should just kill you now," he snapped, his face swathed in shadows as he loomed over her.

Fear punched through her as he started to raise his weapon, but when she heard the word "Quack!" shouted from in front of her, she dove back into the mud without a second thought.

"What the fu—" The man's head exploded as he flew backward.

She shoved up, looking in the direction Chance's shout had come from, to find him running through the mud with ease toward her, a weapon in hand. She was in his arms before she was aware of moving. "Quack?" she managed to get out through a short sob of tears. She tried to swallow it back, because she knew they weren't out of the woods yet—pun intended. And she needed to keep it together until they got all those women and his brother to safety.

Chance kissed her once, hard, before he pulled back. "It just came out." His voice was raspy, his eyes dilated in the dimness as he looked down at her. "I can't believe—"

"Well it worked," she said as she buried another sob, refusing to let it out now. When they gamed together, they used the word "quack" instead of "duck" when warning the other that danger was incoming. And she'd heard it and just reacted on instinct. "Where's your brother and the women?"

"Hopefully across the lake. There's still two more guys out here," he said urgently, turning away from her. "Jump on my back. We'll make better time. When I couldn't get through to you…" She heard the tremor in his voice.

"I took out my earpiece so he wouldn't know I had a partner. I tossed it in the mud."

"I wish I could kill him all over again," he growled, but then seemed to get it together. "I took out two guys in the house," he continued, switching to the more important topic as he reached the tree line near the house once again. Flames licked along the back porch of the house, but the rain was slowly putting it out. "One on the way to the SUV, and then that final guy. That's six including the ones in the explosion," he murmured as he set her on her feet, crouched down and pulled out small binoculars, started scanning the area.

The rain was starting to pull back so that they could see all the way to the lake and down the shoreline. It was still too thick to see if anyone was on the water, but Berlin had heard Chance tell his brother to cross the lake.

"What's the plan?" she asked as he handed her the binoculars. There was one man at the end of a long dock holding up a set of binoculars as he faced the water. "I see one guy."

"There's another one we've gotta find so we're not sitting prey. And I don't want to leave you again." Water dripped down his hair and cheeks as he looked down at her. "Will you shoot a pistol?"

She noticed he said *will you*, not *can you*. "Yeah. I don't love it but it's us or them and we've got to save those women."

He handed her a small revolver tucked away in the back of his pants. "This is my second backup and it's only got six bullets. I want to get close to the shoreline, then head in from the water and take him out," he said as he pulled her back behind a tree for cover. "You can come with me until we reach the tree line closest to the shore, but…"

"I get it. And I've got this." She held the weapon out, glad it was a type she'd practiced with before. "I can hunker down and use the darkness and these big-ass trees to hide. I don't like it, but I understand the necessity."

He shoved out a quick breath. "Okay, let's go. And whatever happens, you stay hidden. If something happens to me, I need you to run and hide, then get help."

She half nodded, but didn't mean it. She wasn't leaving him behind, no matter what.

CHaPTer 29

Out of the frying pan...

Berlin hated waiting for anything, but she really hated waiting as Chance slipped into the dark lake like a ghost, disappearing right before her eyes as he ducked under the murky waters. He'd told her that he planned to swim along the shoreline, using that as his guide since it was too dark to see anything.

That alone was terrifying.

But she remained hidden in the shadows of the trees, only peering out with the binoculars to keep an eye on the man on the dock. The rain had slightly lessened, and he was scanning the turbulent lake, almost seemed to be waiting for something... Oh god, had he called in backup?

But then he turned, striding back down the dock toward the shore in clear frustration. The dock was long, but so were his strides as he hurried toward shore.

Suddenly a shadow erupted from the water, and while she couldn't see what happened, the man cried out, crumpling onto the dock before he was pulled into the water, his head hitting the wooden planks with a sickening thud before he disappeared from sight.

Thirty seconds later, Chance stalked out of the water like an avenging god, dragging the body with him, tossing it into the sand—

"Quietly stand up and don't make a sound or I'll be forced to shoot you in the face." Berlin turned at the sound of a female voice, froze.

It took a second but she recognized the woman from Chance's camera feed before it had gone dark—Nicola. Berlin was glad she'd tucked her pistol into her jacket pocket and hoped the woman wouldn't search her. She slowly pushed up from where she was crouched by the tree, held her hands out.

"Hands down. I know you're working with Enzo's brother. How did you get here?" The woman wasn't wearing a boot on her foot anymore, and was standing normally.

"SUV."

"Take me there now."

"No."

The woman blinked, shoved her pistol at Berlin, but she didn't take a step closer.

"You're just going to kill me," Berlin said, trying to stall.

The woman rolled her eyes. "No, I'm not. I just want to get the hell out of here before backup shows up. And I see your partner," the woman murmured as the rain started to pick back up, lightning forking across the sky in angry slashes. "Move, unless you want me to shoot him."

Berlin wanted to stand her ground but knew she needed to wait for the right moment. She stalked back into the shadow of the woods, the rain pelting Berlin in the face, little pings of pain against her cheeks as she slogged through the mud. As they headed deeper into the woods, Berlin couldn't see the shoreline anymore, couldn't see Chance. But it was clear that this woman was walking just fine, had probably never needed that boot at all. Had she...killed Enzo? Oh god, Berlin shoved that thought down, refused to dwell on it.

"Why are you doing this?" she asked, hoping the woman would give her something.

"I just need a ride out of here, that's all. I'm not going to kill you."

Berlin certainly wasn't going to believe the woman pointing the gun at her. "We're here to help you guys, to get you safety."

The woman gave a bitter, mirthless laugh. "No one can keep me safe."

"Were you ever really being trafficked?" Berlin asked.

Now the woman snorted derisively, the sound eaten up almost immediately by the falling rain. "I'm not one of those women."

As if being a victim was the real crime. "So why are you here?" Berlin had to slide over a fallen log, slipped and fell in the mud.

"Come on, hurry," the woman urged, but at least she didn't shove Berlin. No, she was looking behind her, likely for Chance.

She was wise to be afraid of him.

Berlin pushed back to her feet and kept onward, dreaming of dry clothes, clean fingernails, a warm fire and none of this bullshit. "You're going to kill me anyway. And I'm curious about who you are."

"You know what they say about curiosity," the woman murmured, still clearly distracted. "I work with some men who transport women to the East Coast. Among other things. They didn't trust Enzo—or the man who'd sent him, more accurately—and tasked me with making sure he made the delivery. And they were wise not to trust that little bitch. He has no idea who I am. But I'm using this as an opportunity to leave everything behind and start over." There was a grim determination to her voice.

Berlin had no doubt that the woman herself had suffered, but she was still part of trafficking humans. She wouldn't feel bad for her.

At the sound of a branch breaking behind them, Berlin turned to find the woman had swiveled as well, had her weapon aimed at the darkness.

Berlin slid up behind her, pressed the pistol to her spine. "Drop your weapon now. Or you're never walking again. Don't bend down, just drop it."

The woman sucked in a breath and Berlin swore her own heart stopped for long moments before the woman released the pistol, dropping it into the mud.

Chance stepped out of the darkness then, his own pistol trained on the woman. Berlin felt the energy drain from her in that moment. She wasn't going to fight.

"Is your brother okay? Did you find him and the others?"

Chance nodded just as she heard the sound of... Was that rotor blades in the distance?

Yep.

That was either very good, or very bad.

CHaPTer 30

Patience: what you have when there are too many witnesses.

Chance didn't like any of this, but he especially didn't like that the Feds were now involved. Sitting on the opened back hatch of an SUV, he kept his arm around Berlin's shoulders. They'd been given blankets, but he didn't think they was helping much against the mud and rain that had to have soaked her through to the bone.

Adalyn strode over then with the woman he'd officially met when she'd touched down in an FBI helicopter in a clearing not too far from here, Special Agent Hazel Blake. Her jet-black hair was pulled into a bun at the base of her neck, a wide brimmed hat keeping most of the now drizzling rain off her face.

"This is a giant mess," Adalyn murmured, her jaw tight. "Wish I'd known how many dead bodies were on the ground."

"Or you wouldn't have called me?" Special Agent Blake raised dark eyebrows as she glanced at Adalyn.

"Well, yeah, but I wasn't going to say it out loud."

"It's fine. I've got this...contained."

Chance hadn't said much and neither had Berlin, on Adalyn's orders when she'd arrived in a blaze of glory on that chopper.

"Please explain to me how, because that isn't going to disappear." Adalyn jerked her thumb at the bagged bodies lined up next to a big van with the back doors open.

The agent's expression was relatively neutral as she sighed, but then she looked at Chance. "Like I said, as of right now this is contained to a small group of agents. I trust everyone here. I've also looped in exactly two DEA agents, both of whom I trust."

"Commander Levine one of them?" Adalyn interjected.

Hazel nodded, then looked back at Chance. "You're going to be questioned, and I suggest you get a lawyer. That said, your brother is likely going to be put into WITSEC, along with Nicola Abelev."

"That's her real name?" Berlin asked.

"Apparently," the special agent murmured. "And she wasn't lying to you, she really did work with the Acton brothers. I'm pretty sure she was trafficked herself once upon a time, but either way she seems to know a lot of shit about them and she's willing to talk. She's got names, locations, a whole lot of dirt. She's already given up really great information and said there's more for us if we put her in WITSEC."

"Well that's good," Berlin said, her expression unreadable.

"We're going to bring down a huge operation and cut a big hole in drug and human trafficking from Texas to Georgia. I know some monster will eventually fill the void, but for right now, this will hurt the Becerra cartel. Which brings me to the next topic... I'm going to work it so that your names stay out of this. Or I'm going to try. I honestly don't know if it'll be possible, but I'm going to do everything in my power to keep your names out of this. After what you guys did in Montana," she said, looking pointedly at Adalyn, "Levine has no problem with that."

Chance had no idea what they were referring to and didn't actually care.

His only concern was Enzo and Berlin. "Look, I just want to talk to my brother, and then I really want Berlin to get a shower and dry clothes. She's shivering and the blanket you gave her is shit. She's exhausted and everything else can wait until she gets dry."

Both women blinked at him, but the special agent's mouth quirked up slightly. "All right then, I can do all of that. Come on, let's go talk to your brother."

Chance squeezed Berlin's shoulders once before he strode off with the agent, who took him to where Enzo was sitting on the back of another dark, unmarked SUV.

Enzo slid off as soon as he saw him and Chance's throat tightened when his brother pulled him into a tight hug.

Chance hugged him back, hard, needing to reassure himself that Enzo was alive. Finally they parted as Hazel stepped away, murmuring that she'd give them a few minutes of privacy.

Enzo wiped away wetness on his cheeks. "Thank you for...everything. The last few weeks are surreal, but today..." He shook his head. "I'd be dead without you."

"I'm just glad you're okay."

"I should have called you earlier, but I thought it was too much for you to handle." His gaze strayed to the body bags now being loaded up into a van. "Clearly not."

"I hear you might go into WITSEC?"

"Yeah, at least temporarily. It's a lot to think about but...maybe it's a good thing. Fresh start and all that."

"You don't need WITSEC for a fresh start."

"I know that, but I want to testify against those assholes. And all the women they took are going to testify too. They'll be given asylum if they want and a fresh start. I hope they take it."

"And you had no idea that Nicola woman wasn't who she said?"

"No, but looking back, there were signs. But she had big eyes and a pretty face and I'm apparently a sucker for that. Look...I need to say some things in case I don't get to later. I'm sorry for blaming you for stuff that was out of your control. You were always there for me and Ivy. And you were a kid yourself, just trying not to drown when Mom... Well, you were there, you know what happened. I understand why you joined the army and I'm so proud of you."

Chance cleared his throat, unsure what to say. Finally, he found his voice. "I'm proud of you too. It took guts to go on the run like that. Danny's gonna be pissed about his place," he added, mainly to lighten things.

Enzo let out a sharp bark of surprised laughter. "Yeah, he won't be doing me any favors ever again. He's got to have insurance though. If not, maybe I can convince the Feds to do something about the damage."

Chance had a feeling that Berlin's crew would cover the cost of the damage if he asked and he might do just that. "We'll get it taken care of either way."

"Chance!" Adalyn called out from where she still stood with Berlin, nodded once at him.

"You've gotta go," Enzo said, pulling him in again for another hug.

"I'll figure out a way to get into contact with you. My girl is a genius so if the Feds won't let you call, we'll find a workaround."

"Your girl, huh?"

Chance glanced over at Berlin, still covered in mud, her clothes mostly wet and her hair plastered against her face. He had a feeling she might try to run from him again, but that was okay. She wouldn't get far. "Yep."

"Hopefully I get to officially meet her one day."

"You will." He hugged his brother once more, then jogged over to the others. It was time to get the hell out of here.

CHAPTER 31

We're sisters. If I'm mad at someone, you are too. Rules are rules.

Three days later

Berlin took the beer Chance set in front of her, then curled up against him on the couch as Hazel stepped into her living room. The whole crew, minus Tiago, was already there. And while it was good to be home, she wanted to know where Redemption Harbor Security stood with the Feds and DEA.

And for the last three days it had been radio silence.

"I'm glad you guys are all here." Hazel declined a beer that Rowan held out for her with a shake of her head. "Your brother's doing well," she said, looking at Chance.

He just nodded, his big body vibrating with energy. They'd stayed at the safe house the last two days, then headed over here this morning once they'd gotten a message from Hazel that they were in the clear.

"Will I be able to talk to him before he leaves?" Chance asked Hazel.

"Yep. I've set it up for tomorrow. And I don't think he'll be in WITSEC forever, just until the DEA plugs their leaks."

"Is he safe?" Chance straightened, sitting up on the edge of the couch.

"Yes. A very small team in the marshal's office knows where he's going and that's it. Commander Levine and I have been assigned to a JTF so I, and a few others, are working with a small team within the DEA as we dismantle what's essentially a pipeline of drugs and humans from Texas to the Georgia/South Carolina area and beyond. With the information we got from the Backwater Bayou Boys and the Uptown Street Kings, and Enzo and Nicola...we're cleaning house."

"Are we in any potential danger?" Adalyn asked. "For being involved."

"Your names aren't on any official documents. Officially the Acton brothers who attacked Enzo and the women's hiding spot were taken out by a DEA FAST team. Oh, and we also managed to get Johnny Moore to testify too."

"You guys picked him up?" Berlin couldn't keep the surprise out of her voice.

"Yeah. He was staying with his sister in California. As far as he says—and I actually believe him—he didn't know about the human trafficking. Don't get me wrong, he's not a saint, but he's not complete and total scum. He asked for therapy as part of his relocation package and he's going to be testifying about a lot of stuff, some of it unrelated to the Uptown Street Kings."

"Eh." Berlin shrugged. "He's kind of gross, but I'm glad to hear about the therapy."

Chance shook his head as he slid his arm around her again.

"True enough, but he's got a lot of intel it's clear that he was saving for a rainy day," Hazel said.

"So, about Brody Williams. Are there any parameters to his deal?" Berlin's voice was almost deceptively neutral.

Hazel cocked an eyebrow. "You *know* there are. If he leaves anything out or is less than honest with the prosecutor, then he's going to jail and the offer of WITSEC is withdrawn."

"So if you find evidence that he knew about the trafficking..." Berlin trailed off.

"So far he's claimed that he only knew about the Acton brothers' drug running and their association with the Backwater crew. And I don't have anything to say otherwise."

"Good to know." Berlin had no doubt that scumbag had known about the trafficking and she was going to prove it. But that was for another day.

"All the women you guys saved are also on their way to new homes with new identities. And in two cases, their families are being granted asylum and being moved as well. Unfortunately we're not taking out any cartel members, but we're making a huge dent in their pipeline. The Backwater Bayou crew, the Uptown Street Kings and the Acton brothers are all out of action, hopefully permanently. Which means the Becerra cartel is going to lose a shit ton of money and trust with the people they deal with. This will cripple them so I'm calling a win."

"What about Santiago Alonso? Was he involved with anything?" The grumpy tattoo artist Santi had come up on her radar when she'd searched his face, but it had been minor run-ins with the law when he was younger. Carlos, on the other hand, had been one of the dead guys Chance had killed in Natchez.

"As far as we can tell, no. And after a very short conversation with him, Camila tells me that he's glad the Acton brothers will be moving out of town. He's got no love for law enforcement but he hated those guys, said they ran shit through the tattoo shop but there was nothing he could do about it. Oh, that address you gave us a tip on, the one in Houston, the DEA made a very nice bust there. It was a big hub for the Acton brothers. They had a hacker staying there and he tried to destroy everything before the FAST team busted in, but he wasn't quick enough. Levine is swimming in evidence right now and your biggest fan."

"He said that?"

"Not exactly." Hazel grinned slightly. "But he said he'd buy you a beer any day of the week."

She'd take it. "What about Luis, from the tattoo parlor?" Berlin asked.

"He was definitely involved, but he's low level so he's not on my radar for now. And it looks like he's left town." She shrugged, then glanced at her watch. "I've got a meeting to get to, but I wanted to stop by in person to relay everything. I'm going to be busy for the next couple months but you know you can reach out with anything. And thank you guys, for all you've done."

Adalyn stood and walked out with Hazel as Rowan turned to the rest of them. "First things first, I'm starving and want to grill. Berlin, would you care if I bought you a grill, and Chance and I headed out to grab food for dinner?"

She blinked. "You want to buy me a grill?"

"Yeah. Your place is great but you need a few things."

"Uh, sure, thanks. What's the second thing?"

"Tiago and Fleur finally set a wedding date so I need help planning a big bash. They don't want to do separate bachelor and bachelorette parties."

"And you're asking me for help?" She couldn't keep the surprise out of her voice.

"Oh, god no," he said, turning to look at Bradford and Ezra. "But you two are going to help so consider yourself officially enlisted. You too, Chance, if you decide to stick around."

Ooooh, Berlin wasn't sure how to respond to that and kind of wanted to punch Rowan in the shoulder right now. But since her own shoulder was still healing from being punctured by a stupid stick (the woods *were* stupid!) her range of movement was limited.

Chance cleared his throat slightly, but didn't respond either.

"Jesus, Captain Awkward, way to go." Bradford smacked Rowan as he stood and headed to the connected kitchen.

Thankfully Adalyn stepped back in at that moment, drawing everyone's attention to her.

"Your man needs to be fitted for a muzzle," Ezra called out as he stood as well, stretching his legs.

"I like his mouth very much, thank you, so that won't be happening." Adalyn grinned as she stepped into the living room. "So are we going to eat or what? I'm starving."

"I swear, you two are made for each other." Berlin stood with Chance, ready to start pulling out stuff for a barbeque, then there was a sharp knock on her front door.

She frowned, wishing she had her phone with her so she could check the cameras, but Adalyn was quick, and hurried out of the room... And moments later strode back in with three familiar women in tow.

Berlin blinked in true surprise to see her three sisters there. "Hey guys...is everything okay?"

"Yeah, of course," Sydney answered.

Cheyenne was the only blonde, though they all had the same blue-green eyes of their mom. Sydney and Geneva had the same dark hair as Berlin and their mom. But they all had the same build and same facial features. There was no denying they were sisters.

"We've been calling and you haven't responded," Geneva said.

"I've been texting," she said, feeling a little defensive. The last three days she'd mostly been in bed with Chance. And truthfully, she hadn't wanted to talk to anyone but him after the whole mess at the lake cabin. She'd needed time to mentally digest everything—was still dealing with it.

"Well we missed you so we decided to plan a little road trip," Cheyenne said as she dropped a duffel bag on the ground. "We're going to grab a hotel but—"

"No, you won't do that. I've got the room." Sort of, but Berlin would make it work. "Ah, guys, these are my sisters, officially." She'd talked about them, but they'd never actually met her sisters before.

"And you've got good timing," Rowan said as he held out a hand to Geneva. "We're about to grill burgers and whatever you guys want."

"Ooh, a party, I'm in." Sydney grinned.

"Who are you?" Geneva asked Chance pointedly, maybe because he had his arm looped possessively around Berlin.

Exactly the way she liked him holding her. Berlin felt her cheeks heat up. "Ah, guys, this is—"

"I'm Chance. Berlin's boyfriend."

"Boyfriend?" she blurted before she could order her mouth to stay shut. She really, really liked the sound of that, but they hadn't discussed the future. They'd mostly holed up and had sex. Like on an industrial level. And she wasn't complaining. But still.

"It sounds better than lover." His tone was dry.

She mock shuddered. "Gross, please don't say that."

"Fine, boyfriend it is." He leaned down close to her ear so that only she could hear. "Because I'll never share you. We're not dating other people."

"Boyfriend!" Her sisters practically giggled with glee as they all sized him up.

Seriously, what the hell was happening? She was happy they were here, but couldn't believe they'd just shown up.

"All right, come on," Rowan nodded at Chance, who sighed but kissed Berlin soundly before he headed out with the other guys and Adalyn to apparently go buy her a grill and food, while her sisters stayed behind.

"So, boyfriend? He's gorgeous," Geneva said with a little awe as they all tackled her in a belated sister hug.

Berlin hugged them back, glad all her sisters were here. She was so proud of them, but she missed them all the time and wished they all lived next door so she could see them every day. Since that wasn't reality, she would take this time with them.

"Yeah, holy crap on a cracker," Sydney added as she stepped back, while Cheyenne nodded her approval. "That is a *man* man."

Berlin nodded in agreement. "He is pretty amazing."

"And he looks at you like you hung the moon," Cheyenne said, grinning. "Also, I ended things with Toby for good, just FYI. He's a loser and you were right. I can do better."

"Hell yeah you can," Geneva grumbled.

"Why are you guys really here?" Berlin asked as they all settled on the couches.

"To see you," Cheyenne said. "And I know we should have called, but...you weren't responding to our calls and we got worried you were mad at us or something."

Berlin blinked. "I was texting you! And...Chance and I been kind of occupied the last few days." Her injured shoulder hadn't slowed them down at all. If anything, it had given him an excuse to do all the work, and wow, that was like a drug. The man had her so addicted to him, she was never letting go.

"Oh. Ooooh," Geneva grinned. "Okay then, that's excusable. So tell us what we've missed the last couple weeks."

Berlin couldn't tell them everything and for the most part kept them insulated from her work, but they knew that she was in "investigative" work so she could weave in a few fun details, minus all the killing and gore. But telling them about Johnny was actually funny. And she got to hear about their lives in person, not over the phone or via text or video call.

Being with her sisters filled up something inside her. And even though she knew she needed better boundaries in general, these were always going to be her sisters, women she loved more than anything.

***

Chance wasn't surprised by how much he liked Berlin's sisters, considering she'd practically raised them. And seeing the joy on her face with them around filled him with...he wasn't even sure what. But he loved this woman and he wanted her to be happy all the time.

The love thing had taken him off guard, but it was something he knew to his bones.

He didn't want to just be her boyfriend, but knew he'd have to wait for more. And he could do patience, especially with a woman like Berlin. She was worth waiting for.

Hours later, once everyone except her sisters were gone, he and Berlin were finally alone in her bedroom. She walked out of the bathroom wearing a silky robe and her damp hair in a long braid as she collapsed on the bed next to him. She was already rolling onto his chest as he tucked her in close.

Exactly where she belonged.

"My sisters all like you," she murmured against his chest, exhaustion clearly creeping in as she idly traced her fingers over his scars along his jaw and collarbone.

It was only seven, but he was beyond tired too, ready to crash and not wake again until the sun was up. "I like them too."

"Can we go back to the whole boyfriend thing?"

"What's there to go back to?" He tightened his grip on her, kissed the top of her head. He was ready to get naked, but he didn't think she was up to it. "And how's your arm feeling?" She'd insisted on changing her bandage today by herself. He wasn't even sure why he was annoyed, but he wanted to be the one who took care of her.

"Fine, I guess."

"You could take the meds you were prescribed." It had been simple ibuprofen but she'd rejected even that.

She just made a snorting sound.

"I'll take that as a no."

"So...we're like together?" she asked, rolling back slightly to look up at him.

"Yep." He wasn't going anywhere.

"Well...how will that work? I live here and you live—"

"I'm moving here. I'd planned to talk to you about it tomorrow, but Adalyn asked if I wanted to work for you guys. She said if I was going to take down bad guys, I should at least get paid for it."

Berlin blinked and he realized he'd actually surprised her.

"She didn't tell you?"

"No, that sneak," she grumbled, but smiled. "So what did you say?"

"That I'd have to talk to you about it, to make sure you were on board. Because I don't want to invade your workspace."

"That's really thoughtful."

"Why do you sound so surprised by that?"

She laughed lightly. "I'm not, I swear. I'm just surprised she didn't say anything to me, that's all. And I'd love it if you worked with me. With us. But only if you really want the job."

"I've been drifting since I got out of the army. My only real goal was to find my brother. And so far I like what I've seen. I like what you guys are doing. And...I like working in gray areas." He'd missed that part of his former life more than he'd thought he would.

"Same." She grinned up at him.

He planned to put his grandmother's house up for sale, then split the profits with his brother, who he was still worried about but also proud of. Then he wanted to get a place here—or just move in with Berlin if she'd have him. Leaning down, he brushed his lips over Berlin's, needing to taste her, claim her. "Are you too tired for anything?" he whispered. "You can lie back and let me do all the work."

She snickered against his mouth. "Those are the sweetest words ever. And I'm definitely not too tired, I just need to be careful with my arm."

"I've got you," he murmured, kissing her again. Always.

EPILOGUE

Two months later

"I'm coming, I swear!" Berlin slid her laptop into its case as she heard the elevator door open outside her office.

But to her surprise, Mari stalked in, not Chance, who was taking her on a secret getaway he refused to give her any details about. She didn't have the heart to tell him she hated surprises so she was going along with it. She'd even resisted the urge to sneak and figure out what he was doing.

"Oh hey, I'm heading out," she said to Mari.

"I know, I just saw Chance," she practically growled as she stalked into Berlin's office, prowling toward the window like an angry bear ready to rip off someone's head.

"Uh oh, what's wrong?"

Mari turned to face her, her blue-black hair swishing around her shoulders as rage rolled off her in almost tangible waves. "I want to hire you to destroy someone. Completely obliterate their life."

"I don't really do that, but I might make an exception for you. Who's pissed you off so badly?"

She shoved her hands in her jeans pockets. "You know Bear?"

"I'm not hurting him!" And Berlin was ninety-nine percent this wasn't about Bear anyway. The man was an adorable, well, teddy bear. And Mari had been friends with him since she was fifteen.

Mari rolled her eyes. "Of course not, I *adore* him. It's his stupid, assface older brother. He's moved back to town and is trying to steal one of my newest contracts."

"I thought his brother was in the Air Force... Yep, okay, not the issue at hand. So wait, he's trying to steal one of your contracts?"

"Or sabotage it, I'm not sure which," she growled, looking ready to set fire to something. "I want you to hack his life and burn it to the ground. Then salt the earth." Sighing, clearly losing some of her steam, she continued. "Fine, maybe not that, but only because it would upset Bear. But I do want to punch his dumb face."

"Are you sure you don't want to sit on his dumb face?" Because Berlin was getting some serious vibes right now.

Mari swiveled to look at her, those proverbial daggers in her eyes.

Berlin held up her hands. "Okay, okay, I'm off base. Well if he's messing with your business, why don't you mess right back? You're Mari Freaking Kim, destroyer of worlds. Steal one of his clients—legally. Buy out something he wants. You don't need me to help you, though if you truly do, I'll help once I get back from whatever trip I'm about to take."

Mari's eyes narrowed slightly and Berlin was under the impression that she wasn't even seeing her at all right now. "You're right. I can take him on all by myself." Then she let out a sort of terrifying laugh that made Berlin feel bad for the guy. Well, almost. If he was messing with her girl, then he'd likely earned whatever storm was coming his way. Mari blinked and looked at Berlin with clear eyes. "Thanks for the advice, you're the best. And have fun on your trip," she tossed over her shoulder as she stalked out of the office in the same whirlwind she'd arrived in.

Chance ducked into the office right as she left. "Hey, you ready? And no laptop!" he added when she went to pick hers up.

"Wait, what? I never agreed to that."

"You're not going to need it."

She gently petted the purple and black case, then sighed. "Fine, let me put her in the safe and we'll go. I still wish you'd tell me where we're going."

"I already told you it's a surprise."

"Fine, as long as it's not camping."

***

Chance bit back a laugh as he glanced over at Berlin, who was watching him accusingly from the passenger seat. "You brought me camping!"

"Technically it's glamping, and I *promise* you're going to like this. And...you're going to meet the guys from my former unit," he said as he cruised at fifteen miles per hour along the narrow road, passing another row of hooked-up campers. "This is the only time they're all together and I really wanted them to meet you. I wanted to show you off."

"Oh." She sniffed a little. "I feel like you're manipulating me, but I'll allow it this one time. Also, will there be s'mores?"

"Yes, all the s'mores you want."

"Okay, I guess. But if there are bears, I'm out."

"That's fair." After they passed the six rows of campers, she frowned up at him as he steered down an even narrower path with a sign that said *primitive camping*. "You said glamping. Pretty sure we just passed all the campers, and 'primitive' means tents."

"I would never make you sleep in a tent."

Two minutes later, he pulled into a clearing where twelve huge military tents were already set up in a giant circle, along with one Airstream. It had a cute blue and white awning with a bunch of lights on it. And one of his friends had set up chairs and a couple other things for them.

"The Airstream is ours, right?"

"Yep."

"Okay, I trust you again."

He snickered as he glanced at her, glad she didn't seem truly annoyed. He hadn't been lying—this was the only time his friends had been able to get together and he understood their schedules enough that he had to take advantage of this small window. Because he really wanted them to meet Berlin. Not because he needed approval, but because he truly wanted her to meet them. And fine, he was going to show her off. She was incredible and the world should know.

Before he'd even put the SUV in park, Evan was at Berlin's door, pulling it open. "Okay, my man didn't lie about you," he said as he pulled her into a big hug. "Beauty and brains!"

"And you must be Hot Shot?" Berlin asked with a laugh as he set her back on her feet.

Evan snickered as Chance rounded the vehicle, nudged him out of the way. "Hands off."

Berlin seemed to be smothering another laugh as she slid right up against Chance, wrapping her arms around him.

It didn't take long to introduce her to everyone, and once they'd unloaded their bags, Berlin found herself surrounded by the wives and girlfriends of his former unit around the big campfire.

"Never thought I'd see the day," said Moose, his former team leader, chin nodding in Berlin's direction.

"Never thought I'd meet anyone like her."

Moose clinked beers with him. "I'll drink to that."

The rest of the evening went by in a blur of laughter, beers, and getting to hear his friends tell Berlin way too many stories about him. Some he could have lived without her ever hearing. But he'd wanted to bring her into his world, and if he was being honest, he'd needed to reclaim this part of his life.

After leaving the army he'd felt like he'd lost part of himself, but he was the one who'd put distance between himself and his former unit, not the other way around.

"So being in the woods may not be too bad," Berlin murmured happily and a little sleepily as they stepped into the Airstream. "And you weren't kidding about glamping. This thing is amazing. I could live in it." She ran her fingertips along the smooth countertop in the kitchen before stepping into his embrace.

He had to duck a little because of his height, but it only gave him an excuse to kiss her. Not that he needed one, he thought as he claimed her mouth again. Something he wanted to do all the time. "My friends really like you," he murmured against her lips.

"I really like them too. And I'm really glad we're not sleeping in a tent."

He snickered, then smacked her butt. "Go, shower first. Sadly we can't both fit in there."

"I'm not going to argue about going first," she said with a grin.

Once she'd shut the door behind her, he quickly prepared the bedroom area and then ducked out to take a quick outdoor shower. He knew Berlin would be a while, but he was fast because he wanted to be waiting for her when she got out.

There were a few guys still sitting around the campfire, but the majority of everyone, especially the significant others and kids, were already in their tents and winding down for the night.

Steam billowed out of the shower when Berlin finally stepped out, her long, dark hair up in a twist against the back of her head.

She stared at the bedroom, a smile breaking across her face as she saw the little lights he'd strung up and the small battery-powered candles he'd set out everywhere except the actual bed. "This is really sweet," she murmured, dropping her towel as she joined him on the bed. "And I think you've made me a convert for this kind of camping."

He groaned as she straddled him, clasping her hips to hold her in place. "Wait, just a sec."

"Wait?" She ran her fingers over his abdomen, up his chest, the hungry look in her eyes making him groan.

Sitting up so that they were facing each other, he reached under the pillow, grabbed the box he'd been storing the last month.

"What's that?"

"Just wait." Because maybe he needed a minute too. "I never imagined anyone like you existed, let alone would want someone like me."

"Hey—"

"I know, I know. You don't have to defend me from myself."

But she pouted prettily anyway. And god, it took restraint not to kiss that pout away.

"I just mean that I never expected someone as amazing as you to walk into my life and turn it so thoroughly upside down. Every day since you rolled up and told me to get in that SUV has been an adventure. I love you so much it's a little terrifying." Surprised by how much he was sweating, he pulled the small box out, popped it open. "And I want to keep having adventures with you for the rest of our lives. Will you—"

"Yes." On a laugh, she kissed him hard, sending them tumbling back onto the fluffy comforter.

"So yes, you'll marry me?" he growled against her mouth. Because he needed to hear the words.

"Yes, I'll marry you, anywhere, anytime. I love you so much it's terrifying too. You're incredible, and the only man on the planet I'd try camping for."

Laughing, he pulled her close and held her tight. It didn't take long before they lost themselves in each other, and he knew he'd be losing himself in her for the rest of their lives.

Acknowledgements

As always I owe thanks to my wonderful editor Julia who helps me finetune things. To Tammy, thank you for line edits and always working me in. For Sarah, thank you for all the things (do you get tired of me saying that?). Jaycee, thank for another fabulous cover; I love each cover in the series. To Shelley and the other Tammy, who often send me messages letting me know about typos, I appreciate you both! For my readers, who discovered this world all the way back with the original series and the book, Resurrection. Thank you all for joining me on so many adventures! For my son, who is too young to read my books, and likely wouldn't read this one anyway (because there are no dragons), thank you for all the insight into VR gaming and a world I now somewhat understand. You've taught me a lot about the most random things in the last thirteen years and I'm grateful. Last but not least (never), I'm so grateful to my two pups, Jack and Piper, the best dogs a writer could ask for.

ABOUT THE AUTHOR

Katie Reus is the *USA Today* bestselling author of the Red Stone Security series, the Ancients Rising series and the Redemption Harbor series. She fell in love with romance at a young age thanks to books she pilfered from her mom's stash. Years later she loves reading romance almost as much as she loves writing it.

However, she didn't always know she wanted to be a writer. After changing majors many times, she finally graduated summa cum laude with a degree in psychology. Not long after that she discovered a new love. Writing. She now spends her days writing paranormal romance and action-packed romantic suspense.

COMPLETE BOOKLIST

Saved by Darkness

Guardian of Darkness

Sentinel of Darkness

A Very Dragon Christmas

Darkness Rising

Deadly Ops Series

Targeted

Bound to Danger

Chasing Danger

Shattered Duty

Edge of Danger

A Covert Affair

Endgame Trilogy

Bishop's Knight

Bishop's Queen

Bishop's Endgame

Holiday With a Hitman Series

How the Hitman Stole Christmas

A Very Merry Hitman

All I Want for Christmas is a Hitman

MacArthur Family Series

Falling for Irish

Unintended Target

Saving Sienna

Sworn to Protect

Secret Obsession

Love Thy Enemy

Dangerous Protector

Lethal Game

Secret Enemy

Saving Danger

Guarding Her

Deadly Protector

Danger Rising

Protecting Rebel

Redemption Harbor® Series

Resurrection

Savage Rising

Dangerous Witness

Innocent Target

Hunting Danger

Covert Games

Chasing Vengeance

Redemption Harbor® Security

Fighting for Hailey

Fighting for Reese

Fighting for Adalyn

Fighting for Magnolia

Fighting for Berlin

Fighting for Mari

Sin City Series (the Serafina)

First Surrender

Sensual Surrender

Sweetest Surrender

Dangerous Surrender

Deadly Surrender

Verona Bay Series

Dark Memento

Deadly Past

Silent Protector

Linked books

Retribution

Tempting Danger

Non-series Romantic Suspense

Running From the Past

Dangerous Secrets

Killer Secrets

Deadly Obsession

Danger in Paradise

His Secret Past

The Trouble with Rylee

Falling for Nola

Tempted by Her Neighbor

Falling for Valentine

Paranormal Romance

Destined Mate

Protector's Mate

A Jaguar's Kiss

Tempting the Jaguar

Enemy Mine

Heart of the Jaguar

www.ingramcontent.com/pod-product-compliance
Lightning Source LLC
La Vergne TN
LVHW041129170125
801534LV00002B/428